CASEY COME HOME

SAMANTHA WINSTON

Casey Come Home
ISBN # 978-1-83943-887-5
©Copyright Samantha Winston 2018
Cover Art by Posh Gosh ©Copyright December 2018
Interior text design by Claire Siemaszkiewicz
Totally Bound Publishing

Published in 2020 by Totally Bound Publishing, United Kingdom.

CASEY
COME HOME

Dedication

For Ally, Stef, and sports (and their lovers) everywhere.

Chapter One

The phone rang in the tiny apartment on the third floor. Casey answered it, pushing the shutters open to let in the early morning sun.

"Hello, is this Casey?"

"Yes? Who's calling?" Casey gazed at the sunrise over the tiled roofs of Torino.

"It's me, your ex-tyrannical boss Greta."

Casey chuckled. "You stopped being my boss when I moved to Italy, but you're still a tyrant, I'm sure. Why are you calling me in the middle of the night?" Casey checked her watch. "It must be one a.m. in Ohio."

"I'm up checking the latest edition before it goes to the printers tomorrow and I'd rather call from the office than on my home phone."

"Is anything wrong?" Casey felt a little twinge of disquiet. "Everything's all right back home, isn't it?" She paced as she spoke, walking from the bedroom to the living room.

"Of course, honey. Don't worry. Listen, I have a favor to ask you. I need an interview with a soccer star.

I've set it up for you. Everything is okay. The guy said he'd meet you, no problem."

Casey stopped in the middle of the living room and frowned. "What do you mean soccer? I don't know a thing about the sport. Can't you send Scott to do the interview? He loves sports. I'd sound like an idiot. I don't have the first idea what kind of questions to ask!"

"This is a woman's magazine. We don't want a man's point of view." Greta's sigh sounded loud over the phone. "You're in Italy. You can hop on a bus and be in front of the stadium in half an hour. Another journalist would have to take an airplane, get over her jet lag, check into a hotel and cost the magazine a fortune. You know we're on a budget, Casey. So...please? For a former boss in need of an article about a handsome Italian football star?"

"I thought you said soccer?" Casey resumed pacing. She wanted to help Greta—after all, Greta had been there when she needed her and, besides being her ex-boss, she was an old friend—but she'd never done an interview. She'd make a complete mess of it.

"They call it football everywhere else in the world. We Americans are the only ones who call it soccer. There's a good question for you, 'What do you think about the word *soccer*?' You'll do just fine."

Casey leaned against the window. "Greta, I'm in Italy to study art. And to learn, eventually, how to speak perfect Italian. I am not here to make a fool of myself posing as a journalist."

"You still have your badge, don't you?"

"Well, you gave me one," Casey said. "After all, I did work for the magazine."

"You do have your badge, good. I knew you'd keep it. You just loved to wave that little badge around and get—"

"All right, you win. For old times' sake then. Email me all the details and let's get it over with."

"Thank you, honey. You'll get paid top rates, don't worry about that."

"I should hope so. Now hang up, email me and don't forget to spell the names and addresses right or I'll interview an Italian street cleaner and send you that instead. I'll make up a bunch of lies and you'll get sued."

Greta laughed. "Threats, that's what I get? I go out of my way to find you a job and that's all you can say?"

"I appreciate it. Besides, my art classes don't start until September." Casey pressed her hand against the windowpane. The sun had warmed it. She pulled back and turned away.

Greta's voice was sympathetic. "I'm sure you made the right decision, honey. And, you know, if you wanted to send us articles about your new life, we'd print them. You could write about your neighborhood, the schools, the food and the traditions. I think our readers would like that, we could call it, 'An American in Torino, My Story', what do you think?"

"I think I'll wait for your email. Bye, Greta. It was good hearing from you. I'll keep in touch."

Casey put the phone back in its cradle and walked over to the window in her bedroom. The sun bathed the room in its milky light. It was early. Tucked in the eaves, the pigeons were still sleeping. She shrugged out of her bathrobe and stood naked for a moment in a patch of sunlight. Humming, she went into the bathroom and took a shower. Once dressed in jeans and a T-shirt, she put her damp hair into a chignon and wandered back to the window.

It was late August in Italy and most people were at the coast for their vacation. The city was almost empty — there wasn't the usual hubbub of rushing cars and horn-beeping taxis rattling through the cobblestone streets around the plaza where Casey rented a small, one-bedroom apartment.

Now the pigeons were starting to coo in the eaves. There was the faint sound of a train leaving the station, and a woman down on the street was sweeping her stoop.

Casey leaned against the windowsill and stared out at the scene. Torino was renowned for its beauty and splendid architecture and it boasted many famous churches, parks and museums. Torino wasn't one of the quaint Italian cities with the red-tiled roofs and medieval houses. It was a magnificent city, built on the site of an ancient fortified castle on a plateau surrounded by the Piedmont Mountains. The remains of the castle and the outline of the walls were still visible, but the city had grown and sprawled around it, hiding the old outline and blurring it, so that you'd never believe kings and armored knights had once ridden along the banks of the wide Po River.

Casey hummed as she put coffee into the percolator and cut bananas onto a plate. She'd go get some pastries too, fresh from the bakery just across the street where she bought bread, croissants and the crispy, buttery, almond biscuits she adored. Then she would watch TV, trying to understand the staccato Italian.

Her phone buzzed, startling her. Before she read Greta's email, she wiped her hands on the dish towel and poured herself a cup of fresh coffee. Then she sat on her couch. The email gave her a name, the time of the interview, the address and a few sample questions. The magazine had been bombarded with letters ever since it had covered the World Cup in Paris. Most of the letters had to do with the Italian soccer team and Casey was amused to see that Greta had included a few letters in the email.

Dear Watch Out! *I really enjoyed your articles about the World Cup, and the photos of the players. Who'd have thought soccer babes were so cute? I'm looking forward to seeing more stuff on soccer, especially about the Italian team! Where do they usually play? Where can we see them?*

Dear Watch Out! *I love soccer! I play on our school team, on our county team and on our club team. I want to become a pro and would appreciate some tips. Is it true that in Europe women don't play soccer?*

Dear Watch Out! *Please don't let the World Cup finals spell the end of soccer in your magazine. I think your sports section should give equal space to all sports, not just the American ones. What about articles on individuals? We know how the American sports superstar lives – how does the rest of the world treat their stars?*

Casey jotted down a few ideas then checked the date again and swore – it was for that afternoon. *Damn!* And the name – *A. Salamander*, but that couldn't be right, could it? She ran her hand through her hair and muttered under her breath, then she put on her shoes and went to get her almond pastries.

In the *panificio*, the baker greeted her by name, a wide smile on his shiny face. His wife, working the cash register, squeezed Casey's hand and told her how pretty she looked that morning. Casey, still not used to the Italian show of affection and emotion, smiled, nodded and managed to escape from the crowded shop with her breakfast.

As Casey had soon discovered, in Italy everyone spoke to everyone—on the street, in the market, in the apartment and in the neighborhood. It hadn't taken long before everyone on her street knew about the American widow who lived in number twenty-one. The women all clucked their tongues when they spoke to Casey, they put their hands on her arms and squeezed. They all knew she was an artist, and she'd yet to meet an Italian who didn't profess a fondness for art. They'd also learned that she wanted to go to the international cooking school and that seemed to amuse them.

"Do all Americans need to study cooking in Europe?" they asked. "What do they know? Hamburgers?"

Casey had explained that the cooking school was for recreation only, but the art was serious, and anyone who wanted a portrait painted of their children, pets or favorite scene could knock on her door. Business was brisk. She charged reasonable rates and flattered subtly. The neighborhood adopted her as their own token American. And today she had to go interview a real, live Italian soccer star.

* * * *

Casey stared in dismay at the stadium. It was huge. She'd never been near it, always staying on her side of the river in the older section of the city.

There was a crowd around the door. She was aware of the importance of soccer in Torino. She knew that the team was the Italian version of the Super Bowl victors. They had won or been in the finals each of the eight years running. The team was on posters and T-shirts all over the city. The whole city dressed in white, the team's color, for every match. There were even magazines devoted to the soccer team called the Squadra di Torino, known as the *squadra bianca* because of its white shirts.

The taxi driver was so impressed she was going to interview one of the players he almost forgot to charge her. He also decoded the name on the email, raising his eyebrows and saying "Alessandro!" with considerable awe. Casey deduced that the Alessandro in question was some player.

Casey chewed on her pencil and wished she knew the first thing about soccer, or that she'd taken the time to watch a whole game. She never had. She'd meant to – she was always starting to watch, then getting up to do the dishes, read or take a bath. Her neighbor's son was nuts about soccer – maybe she should have taken him with her. All her neighbors were soccer fans – she could have asked anyone between the ages of three and a hundred and three and they would have been able to explain the rules to her.

Well, it was too late to fret about it now. With a sinking heart, she made her way toward the huge crowd. She didn't think she'd even make it through. "Excuse me, I need to get by" didn't make a dent. Finally she noticed another guarded entrance. Pushing and shoving, she made her way to the sentry, brandished her pass and was let in, to the dismay of fifty or so shrieking fans.

Once in the dark, echoing corridor, she leaned against the wall and took several deep breaths. Pummeled, battered and squashed, she checked her backpack to make sure she still had everything. Then she found the elevators and sighed with relief. She had an appointment in the pressroom in fifteen minutes, time to get herself together and, with luck, meet another journalist who could help her.

* * * *

The pressroom was enormous, lit by harsh, white neon lights and boasting desks with outlets for journalists to plug in their laptops. Some were drinking coffee near a dispenser. Casey smiled and said hello, but the greetings returned by the men were distracted. They eyed her but didn't make any efforts to help her. She bit her lip and tried again.

"Excuse me, I have an appointment with one of the players. Supposedly he's to meet me here, but I don't have any idea who he is and I won't recognize him. Could one of you help me?"

A tall man disengaged himself from the small group and smiled at Casey. "You are American!" It was a statement, not a question, and Casey nodded. "Who is your victim?" he joked. At least Casey hoped he was joking.

"Here's his name, Alessandro Sottini. Do you know him?"

The man's eyebrows rose. "Of course, he is one of the best players. Lucky you! How did you get the interview? Usually he's too busy to speak to us. He has his own column in the sports paper here and he likes to write his own articles. He also has a question and answer forum in the *Squadra di Torino Soccer News*."

Casey stared at the man. "You're kidding," she said.

"Nope, not kidding. But not to worry, he's quite the playboy. He'll answer your questions and probably ask you out to dinner." He shrugged. "Or maybe not. Most of the time it's the women throwing themselves at him. He can't even take a walk in the street without being mobbed. He only goes out with a bodyguard."

Casey grabbed a pen and jotted that down "Are you American? Your English is perfect."

"I'm half-American. My father came over during World War II and fell in love with my mother. They're still happily married," he added with a grin. "What's your excuse for being here? Are you the new correspondent for *Sports Illustrated*? They finally got the right idea, sending a sexy lady instead of a hulking ex-football player to interview a soccer star? I'm sure you'll get much more from the interview than the last guy they sent."

"No, I'm freelancing for a women's magazine."

"A women's magazine." The journalist shook his head. "Amazing. My name's Ilario, by the way, pleased to meet you. I work with the Channel Three news station here as their sports specialist."

"I'm Casey. The pleasure's all mine." Casey shook hands with Ilario then pulled out the list of questions she'd prepared. "Will you please tell me what you think of these? I have never even seen a soccer game," she added in a whisper.

Ilario looked shocked. "Never? What on earth—" His words were cut off by a bustle from the hallway. With an apologetic shrug, he handed the questions back to her. "Good luck, Casey, I've got to go. I hope to see you around. Give me a call if you need any help." He fished in his vest and drew out a card, handing it to her with a flourish. "My professional card with my private number. I'd love to hear from you soon." With that, and a wink, he left, calling to his assistants to follow him.

Casey looked at the card. *Ilario de Baldini.* She tucked it into her pocket then took out her notebook, hoping the familiar sight of it would steady her nerves. *What did Greta get me into?*

"Miss Atter?" The voice came from the doorway as a man entered, wearing a warm-up suit in the black and white colors of the Squadra di Torino.

"Hatter," she corrected, brushing her hair out of her eyes with the back of her hand. "Are you Mr. Salamander?" She closed her eyes. Had she just called him that? It was a slip of the tongue. She'd thought of him as Salamander since this morning. Now he'd turn around and walk out on her, and it would serve her right. "Uh, I mean, Mr. Sottini." She opened her eyes, hoping her cheeks weren't crimson.

He was looking at her from beneath ridiculously long eyelashes that framed extraordinary light amber-colored eyes. He didn't look too angry. She ventured a weak grin.

"You can call me Alessandro," he said, with a charming smile. "It does sound a bit like Salamander, doesn't it?"

"I'm very sorry," she said. "Please call me Casey."

"Casey?" He made a face. "A strange name for a woman... Is it a nickname?"

"It's short for Cassandra."

"Cassandra and Alessandro," he said, a grin on his face. "We'd better not get married, it would be too much of a tongue twister."

Casey's smile slipped. "That's all right," she heard herself saying, "I have no intention of getting married."

He raised an elegant eyebrow. "What a pity. Well, now that we have that clear, what did you want to ask me for your ladies' journal?" His voice was halfway between mocking and courteous, but his eyes had flashed at her tone of voice.

Casey didn't blink. She was used to men asking her out, trying to pick her up and flirting with her. Most of the time, she managed to be polite, but today she was on edge and flustered for some reason. She looked at her notes. "I have a list of questions. I hope you'll bear with me. I have never once sat through an entire soccer game."

"I beg your pardon?"

Casey tilted her head. "First question, how old are you?"

He lowered his chin, looking at her with his uncanny eyes. Finally he said, "I don't think this is going right. I believe I will go back to the field and continue my exercises. I have to do two more hours today, plus the practice with the team. I have already wasted fifteen minutes of my time and my days are short enough as it is."

Casey's cheeks burned. She flipped her notebook closed, trying to appear calm, but her hands betrayed her and it fell on his foot, pages fluttering and slithering right and left.

She lunged at the papers, colliding with Alessandro as he bent to help her. Sitting back, she rubbed her shoulder. "Sorry," she muttered as they gathered papers.

He picked up a few, turning them over and staring at them. "What is this?" he asked. "Did you do these?"

She nodded. "Actually, I'm not a journalist."

"I never would have guessed," he joked, then he grew serious. "You're an artist. These are excellent. Is this the view from your apartment?"

"Yes." She stuck her hand out for the papers he held.

He ignored her, shuffling through them and picking out another. "Who is this?"

"My husband," she replied. "May I have them back, please?"

"Hold on." He tilted his head, looking at the picture, then at her. "What does your husband do? Is he in Italy for his work? Did you accompany him to Europe like the good little wife? How old are you, by the way?"

"That is none of your business."

"So you expect me to answer all your questions but you won't answer any of mine?" His tone turned mocking now.

Casey looked away. She had thought she was angry, but she realized it was embarrassment. She smoothed the papers he handed her and put them in the notebook. "I'm sorry," she said, after a minute. "We've started this all wrong."

"We?"

"I started off all wrong." She forced a grin. "To answer your question, I'm twenty-five years old."

"And your husband's job?"

"He di... He's de..." The words wouldn't come. She broke off and stared at the wall. "I'm a widow." It occurred to her that she had never had to answer that question since Daniel had died. No one had asked her about him. Either they had known and had avoided speaking about him, or they had been told, in low whispers, all about it by her friends. She was still staring at the wall when Alessandro moved in front of her.

"I'm sorry." He took her hand in his. "Was it recent? Tell me about him," he said, drawing her to a chair and settling her in it. He perched on a stool at her feet, looking at her face, her hand still in his.

Casey's face twisted. "He died two years ago. We had been married for four years. He was my high-school sweetheart. Excuse me, but I have trouble talking about him," she said, getting to her feet and slipping her hand from his grasp. Her hand tingled where he'd touched it.

"No, no, not at all. You're doing wonderfully. What was he like?" The question was gentle.

Casey shook her head. "He was very calm, and always serious. He had dark blond hair and blue eyes. He loved nature… His hobby was fly fishing."

"He fished for flies?" Alessandro wrinkled his nose. "How interesting."

"No, it means he fished for trout, with flies." Casey laughed.

"I know, I'm just teasing. You needed to smile."

Casey looked at him. "I suppose you're right," she said with a sigh. "I'm sorry. Can we start over again, please?"

He looked at his watch and shook his head. "No, I really can't."

Casey nodded. "That's all right. It was nice meeting you, Mr. Sottini, anyway. I hope your team does well this year."

"What about after practice? Can you meet me tonight for dinner?"

"Dinner?" Casey gaped at him.

Alessandro's mouth quirked. "Did you think I was going to let you get away so easily? I said dinner, now you have to say, 'I'd love to, thank you,' and then I say, 'Great, I'll pick you up at eight.' Then you give me your address and we do the interview over a wonderful meal. What do you think?"

"I don't know." Casey glanced around. The other journalists were coming back into the room now, all of them glancing at Alessandro with professional interest.

"Hurry, in a moment I won't be able to get away." He sounded tense.

"All right, tonight at eight, number twenty-one, via Bianca."

Alessandro grinned. "That wasn't so hard now, was it?"

Before she could answer, he was gone, dodging the journalists' questions as he ducked out of the door.

Alessandro jogged down the corridor to the locker rooms. Along the way, he greeted people he knew, and Francisco, his trainer, waved and motioned that he needed to talk to him. Alessandro nodded and slipped past the guard into the locker room.

"How are you, Alex?" the guard asked.

"Not too bad, Georgio, not too bad." He'd been saying the same words now for years. *How long have I been here?* It seemed like a lifetime.

Behind his chair, on hangers, were his street clothes. Raul the valet always made sure everything was clean, pressed, and that his jacket and trousers were on hangers in his locker. Raul even polished their shoes while they played. Alessandro's loafers gleamed from beneath the chair.

He sat on the chair and rubbed his knee absentmindedly. His eyes were open, he was staring at the door to the showers, but all he could see was a pale face surrounded by a mass of waving hair, the color of which he'd never seen before. The woman, Cassandra — no, Casey — had the most unusual coloring. Her hair was ash blonde, pale streaked with dark like polished wood. She was not very tall, but she had curves in all the right places. Her eyes were honey-brown with a gray rim around the iris and she had arching eyebrows. She wouldn't be called beautiful by modern standards — her mouth was too small and her chin too pointed. She looked more like a Renaissance beauty. A woman who would grace the walls of a church and make the monks want to break their vows of celibacy.

He rubbed his hand over his forehead. "What am I thinking?" he muttered.

"What's that?" Fabricio, the goalie, came into the room and flopped onto the chair next to him. "I saw you in the interview room," he said and gave a low whistle. "Was that a journalist, or one of your admirers?"

"A journalist," Alessandro replied.

"Maybe she'll want to interview me." Fabricio leered at him. "I'd be glad to tell her all my secrets."

Alessandro threw his towel at him. "Forget it, I saw her first."

"She doesn't look like your type," said Fabricio, eyebrows raised.

"True," said Alessandro. "But I've never had much luck with 'my type'. Maybe I'd better try something else." He'd always dated thin, glamorous actresses or model types—for the most part blind dates fixed up by his press agent. The women giggled and fawned over him. One had been so nervous she hadn't been able to stop talking the whole evening. This woman, Casey, had mispronounced his name, had never seen or heard of him before and when he'd mentioned marriage — *why had that slipped out?* —she hadn't batted an eye. Most other women would have swooned.

"Well, all I can say is if it doesn't work out, give her my number and tell her I'm ready to spill my guts to the first journalist who will listen." Fabricio looked closer at Alessandro. "Hey, I'm only kidding. Don't glare at me like that. You'll curl my hair."

"You're bald," said Alessandro, with a small laugh.

"That's true. See you tomorrow, Romeo."

* * * *

Alessandro waited until the showers were empty before taking his. Then he dressed and bade the staff good evening. His chauffeur was waiting in his parking spot—another part of the stadium guarded from the public. He was able to slip out unnoticed but for a few die-hards who had waited for hours to catch a glimpse of him. He waved at them and leaned back in his seat. "I'm taking a woman to dinner tonight, Tonio," he said to his chauffeur.

Tonio nodded. "Shall I make reservations at the Pescatorii?"

"Please," said Alessandro.

"How was the practice?"

"Tiring."

"Where to, boss?"

"I have to go see Francisco—he wants to talk to me about something. He'll be at the sports club. That won't be long so you can wait in the car. Then I have to go to the television studio to tape a show. It shouldn't last more than an hour. I'll call you when it's over, all right?"

"You're the boss," said Tonio. "Did you eat lunch today?"

"No. I'll grab something at the club. Stop worrying, Tonio, I'll eat a big dinner, all right? Now be quiet, I want to rest." He closed his eyes. When he did, he saw the American woman's face. He wondered if she would like the restaurant, and if she liked Italian cooking. He frowned as a worrying thought jarred him. *What if she changes her mind and doesn't come?*

* * * *

Casey put her things away and ran her hand through her hair, trying to tame it. It was useless. It was always slipping out of its barrette or elastic band and no chignon could hold it for long.

She saw Ilario and waved. He waved back and came over. "So, how did it go?" he asked.

"Terrible," she said, zipping up her bag. "I didn't get a single picture, he didn't answer a single question and I have the definite feeling I was manipulated from the beginning to the end."

"Ah, he invited you out to dinner." Ilario nodded. "His moves are as predictable as the hands of a watch."

Casey took a deep breath. "I'll keep that in mind. Honestly, what else could I do? At least tonight maybe he'll answer some of my questions."

"Look, if you want to avoid the most obvious ones, why don't you read one of the back issues of *The Squadra di Torino* magazine. You can find one devoted solely to him without any problem. Then you'll know things such as his date of birth, where he spent his childhood, how he started playing and where he played as a junior. It will make things a bit easier for you."

"You're right, thanks. Where can I find back issues?"

"In the media room of the public library here in Torino."

"Of course. Thank you again, Ilario. I'm going there right away."

"Can I drop you off?"

"No, I'll grab a taxi."

"I'm heading in that direction." He shrugged. "You won't be putting me out of my way."

Ilario had a tiny Fiat parked just outside. He put his bag into the trunk and held the door open for Casey, saying with a low bow, "Madame's coach awaits her."

She scrunched into the car, setting her backpack on the floor and fastening her seatbelt. Experience had taught her that Italians were the scariest drivers in the world. Ilario was no exception. He drove with one hand on the wheel and the other outside his car. He gesticulated with it — waving at friends, shaking his fist at taxis and reckless pedestrians — or rested it on the roof. It was an odd way to drive, but everyone drove the same way — one hand out of the window, the other on the steering wheel. Casey wondered if the passengers covered their eyes and prayed to whichever little saint dangled from the rearview mirror. Ilario had a little plastic St. Christopher.

When they arrived in front of the library, Casey thanked Ilario and grabbed her bag.

"What, in such a hurry to leave?"

"The library will close any minute," she said, worried.

"If you want, I'll take a look at your questions."

"You don't have to do that."

"No, I insist," Ilario said. "I can't have you making a fool of yourself tonight on your big date."

Casey gave him a sharp look. "I beg your pardon?"

He had the grace to blush. "Sorry. Professional jealousy. He's never asked me out to dine."

She laughed as she opened her notebook and handed him the list. "I'm very sorry for you. Perhaps you need to do something with your hair."

"Very funny. Let's see... You can do away with questions one through nine, keep ten, eleven, twelve, and forget about the rest." He tossed it back at her.

"That bad, huh?"

"Worse," he said with a grin. "Go in the side door of the library. Give the concierge my card. With that, you can get into this place any hour of the day or night. Professional advantages, which I am not loath to share."

"All right. I can take a hint. What is the big question you want me to ask Alessandro for you?"

His eyes sparkled. "I want to know exactly how much he was offered to play in Barcelona and why he refused. I would like to have his opinion of instant replay for the referees, and of the idea that fouls can be sanctioned after a viewing by a special panel of judges, even after the games. Ask him if he thinks soccer coaches make the teams, or if the players do. Oh, and try to find out what happened to Gloria, his latest fiancée."

"That makes four or five questions," Casey laughed, but she jotted them down, raising her eyebrows a bit when he mentioned the fiancée. "Do you think I need to talk about his private life?" she asked.

"If he answers, fine, if not, well…" He shrugged. "Call me tomorrow whatever happens."

Casey got out of the car and stood by his window. "I won't forget. Thank you so much, Ilario. I really appreciate this." She shook his hand then stepped back and waved as he drove off with squealing tires.

* * * *

The concierge glanced at Ilario's card, nodded to her and showed her in. "You can use the green room for reading and taking notes," he told her, "but stay out of the main reading room after hours. The reference materials must be put back in their places, but if you're in a hurry, the books can go in this cart here. The librarian is still here, but the cleaning crew will be in soon, so you'll have a bit of noise."

Wandering through the aisles, Casey soon located several stacks of soccer magazines and started to peruse, stopping to check dates or when a photo caught her eye.

Alessandro was all over the magazine, as Ilario had predicted. His column was a question and answer one, with a short paragraph to give the theme for the next issue. That way he directed the tone of the questions, keeping the page concentrated and professional.

Casey was impressed. She didn't know if he read all the letters sent to him, or if he even wrote the answers himself, but his photo looked good on the upper right corner. In one article, he also appeared dressed in a black-tie outfit at some television gala. On his arm was a beautiful woman in a dress dripping with sparkling sequins. There were pictures of him and his teammates playing a game against their archrivals, Milan AC, and there was a big, pull-out centerfold with the entire team posing with the European Cup. Very interesting indeed.

From the articles, she learned that he was one of the best offensive players the Squadra di Torino had ever had. He'd started playing soccer as a child, rising in the club rankings, going from junior league to the seniors before he even finished high school. She looked in vain for some shred of evidence that he'd been educated, but found only the names of the various clubs he seemed to have grown up in. His family drew the same blank, except for claiming he was 'very close' to his parents. He had been in a soccer school from the time he was twelve and he'd signed his first professional contract on his sixteenth birthday.

Now, seven years later and according to the magazine, he was engaged to an actress, a model and a woman racecar driver—three possible fiancées, if you believed the articles. He was the captain of one of the world's richest soccer teams and he lived like a recluse in Torino, with no hobbies, no other interests that she could find and no life, really, other than soccer.

Casey jotted down dates and tidbits of information for Greta's magazine, thanking the stars for Ilario's advice. She was so involved with the article she was busy writing that she forgot about the time. When the cleaning crew left, dragging and clanging their galvanized buckets behind them, she glanced up from her paper.

"Oh no!" she cried, catching sight of the clock on the wall. She had less than an hour to get back home, take a shower and dress for dinner with the man whose photographs she'd been contemplating.

She got a taxi, told him to hurry then regretted it as he flew around the plaza, looking over his shoulder and pointing out the sights to her at the same time.

"Please," she gasped. "Look at the road!"

"That's the Duomo, and over there, whoops! Idiot!" he yelled out of the window, shaking his fist. "Over there is the cathedral where — watch your own car, you maniac! Where did you learn how to drive? Sorry, where was I? Oh, here's your street." He screeched around the corner and slammed on the brakes. "Are you still there?"

Casey peered over the back seat. "Am I still alive?" she asked.

"Ah, you Americans, always joking. I love your comedies, so funny! Jerry Lewis and Eddie Murphy, so great, no? That will be four thousand and fifty lire, *grazie, grazie mille!*"

"*Ciao,*" said Casey, handing him the bills. Then she toppled out of the cab and staggered up her stairs.

She took a quick shower and pulled on a black skirt. She had a white linen blouse to go with it. It was her all-purpose outfit. With jewelry and high heels, it became dressy, and with white sandals it was casual. She had no idea if she should be chic or not, so she compromised, slipping into the sandals and clipping on heavy gold earrings. She took a black silk shawl in case it was chilly and put her notebook and pen in her black evening bag. She'd just had time to dash pink lipstick across her mouth and put eyeliner around her eyes when the doorbell rang.

She took a last look at her reflection in the mirror. She wasn't glamorous, but then again, she wasn't vain about her appearance, except when it came to her hair. A large gold barrette held it back but tendrils escaped, floating around her temples and tickling the back of her neck. Her husband had loved her hair, the way it gleamed, with streaks of alternating dark and pale. He'd never let her cut it, begging her to leave it long.

She turned her face away from the mirror. She didn't want to go on a date. She had never dated anyone but her husband. All of a sudden, she regretted giving her address to Alessandro. She had the strongest urge to ignore the doorbell, to hide in the apartment and not come out ever again.

Ring! The bell chimed, insisting.

Casey ran her hands over her hair, smoothing it one last time. She had to stop hiding from the world. Life went on. Everyone said that, repeating it to her until Casey thought she'd scream.

Ring!

"I'm coming!" she called, grabbing her purse from the table and throwing the shawl over her shoulders. "Just a second." In front of the door, she took a deep breath, squared her shoulders and said to herself, "Don't be a coward, Casey. Life goes on. Now, go out and live it!"

Chapter Two

She opened the door, expecting to see Alessandro. Instead, a tall, large-boned man with reddish hair and dark glasses stood on the threshold. He was wearing a black blazer and gray slacks. It took Casey a minute to realize he held a chauffeur's hat in one hand. "I've come to pick you up for Mr. Sottini," he said.

"Oh." Casey was nonplussed. "Does he always send his chauffeur? Doesn't he usually pick up his own dates?"

"Yes. No. His car is waiting in the street. Come."

Casey made a face then followed the man down the three flights of stairs to the street where a black Mercedes was parked on the curb. Its windows were tinted so no one could see who was inside. When the man held open the door, she saw the car was empty.

"Where is Mr. Sottini?" she asked, hesitating.

"He's waiting at his apartment. We'll pick him up there."

Casey shook her head and backed away. "I'm sorry," she said, her nerves getting the better of her and her temper slipping. "I'm afraid I won't be going with you. Tell Mr. Sottini that if he wants to see me, he can come get me himself." She was afraid to look at the man as she spoke. Her cheeks were burning and she was sure she was bright red. Instead, she spun around on her heels and started back to the apartment.

"Miss Casey." The man touched her arm. "Please. It's not an insult—sending me, I mean. But you must understand, he can't just go out in public like that." He snapped his fingers. "He has to be careful. If someone sees him, they scream his name and come over to him, begging for autographs, trying to touch him. Then more people start to gather and soon there is a riot. Your street is not a very quiet one. There is a bakery, a video shop, a produce stand and a butcher over there. If he were in the car, it would be mobbed right now. I wouldn't even be able to pull away from the corner."

"I apologize," said Casey, her cheeks heating as she blushed. "I didn't mean to upset you and I certainly never imagined that Alessandro was so popular."

He took off his dark glasses. "He's a soccer star in Italy! You can't get more popular. My name is Tonio Verdi, by the way. I'm Mr. Sottini's chauffeur and bodyguard."

"Pleased to meet you." Casey stuck out her hand.

He grinned and shook it. In his mighty paw, her hand looked small and fragile—Tonio was a big man. "Please make yourself comfortable," he said, opening the door. "I promise I won't drive too fast."

"How did you know I was going to ask you not to?" Casey was bemused.

"I have chauffeured Americans before. You are all timid passengers," he said, putting on his black chauffeur's cap and pulling into traffic.

Casey settled into the soft leather seat and watched the back of Tonio's neck as he drove through the old city. He took the riverside drive that led through the historical part of town where old buildings were lovingly restored then to a more modern area where brand-new apartment buildings rose high into the gray air.

They stopped in front of a tall, white edifice. It was a chic apartment building with large balconies full of myriad flowers and a manicured park surrounding it.

"Here we are." Tonio took off his hat and peered through the windshield. "As you can see, there is a crowd around the front door, waiting for a glimpse of one of their idols."

"Do many famous people live here?" asked Casey, looking with a worried frown at the group of perhaps twenty men and women milling near the entrance. A stern guard kept them all at bay, but they were armed with papers and cameras and some waved little white squadra flags.

"Three soccer stars live in this building. There is Alessandro, an English player with his wife and children and our goalie, the great Fabricio. There is also a television star—a very sexy man who acts in a soap opera."

"Oh," said Casey, rather hoping she'd catch a glimpse of the television star. "What do we do now?"

"We wait. Alessandro will try to sneak out the back. Sometimes it works and sometimes it doesn't." Tonio shrugged. "Unless you want to go get him," he added with a smirk.

Casey stared at him. "You're joking," she said.

"Yes. If they saw you with him, the women would probably want to tear your hair out and there would be twelve photos of you in tomorrow's paper with the words '*Alessandro's fiancée*' splashed over the cover."

Casey was silent, contemplating everything she'd learned today about Alessandro. She didn't know what he thought about his life, but she wouldn't be able to deal with it. For a second, she even pitied him. Then she shook her head. Pity, why? He wanted this life – he'd worked hard for it. He might even love it. That it seemed terrible to her didn't mean he felt the same way.

The door opened and Alessandro slid in, ducking his head close to her knees and yelling at Tonio, "Go!"

"How did you get away?" Tonio asked, pulling out of the parking lot with a screech of tires.

"I paid Fabricio to go down before me and I waited until he was mobbed. He's giving autographs now." He looked upward and flashed a white grin at Casey. "Good evening. Sorry about all this. It's worse right now because the playoffs are next month, but things calm down after that. I like your shawl," he added.

"Thank you," she said, moving her legs away from his face.

Up front, Tonio chuckled. "I had a hard time persuading her to come with me. In my opinion, she's playing hard to get."

Casey choked. "I had no intention –"

"I didn't ask for your opinion, Tony," said Alessandro, sitting up, taking her hand and pressing it to his lips. "You look ravishing," he told her.

His touch sent tingles down her spine. Troubled, she pulled her hand away. "Please," she said.

"Please what?"

"Oh, nothing," Casey said, flustered.

Alessandro leaned back and stretched, showing off a lean torso. "I'm sore. Today we had a practice game and one of my opponents tackled me roughly. I think I sprained my knee during the second practice session," he said, wincing as he rubbed it.

"How does it feel now?" Tonio surprised Casey with the concern in his voice.

Alessandro shook his head and smiled. "Holding together. Don't worry. It'll hold until the end of the season." He turned to Casey. "I made reservations at my favorite restaurant, I hope you like seafood."

She returned his smile with a frown and felt embarrassed to be acting so churlish. What was the matter with her?

Alessandro didn't seem to notice. Instead, he asked her about her art, praising the drawings he'd seen earlier. "You should see them, Tonio, they are truly wonderful. I want to buy some for my apartment. Will you sell me them? I know nothing about art," he went on, "but I know what I like. I love the simplicity of your lines and the way you show light and shadow. Sketches are easier for me to understand than paintings. So often, I feel foolish when confronted with a painting. I miss the artist's message completely. I feel more at home with Renaissance art. It has its symbols and hidden messages, but at least I can recognize people and animals. In modern art, I'm never sure if I'm looking at an object or the manifestation of an artist's nervous breakdown." He gave her a rueful grin. "You must think I'm ignorant. I love art, but know little about it. Perhaps you can tell me what I'd like to know."

Casey gaped at him. She opened her mouth, shut it, then said, "What do you want to know?"

"When you sketch, is it instinctive or is it mostly technique?"

Casey tilted her head to the side, considering. "It's both," she admitted. "I draw because I must. It's an impulse I can't control but I need the technique to do it well. Anyone can draw and a solid technical background can free your creativity. There are rules you must know in order to break them."

"For example?" he asked, curious.

"Well, Michelangelo was perfectly acquainted with the human anatomy. He knew how many muscles a man has in his back. However, to emphasize strength or action, he would draw more muscles than necessary or change their shape to create movement and power. To break rules, one must know them well. Art is simply instinct married to technique, and then set free."

"I feel a bit the same way about soccer." Alessandro smiled at her. "I play because I must. It is something I was born wanting to do, but I had to learn technique in order to surpass myself. Is that what you mean?"

"Yes." Casey was surprised at the comparison. "Although I hope you don't have the same feeling about the rules," she said to him, smiling.

"No, I try to stay well within the rules," he said. The he stared out of the window and they finished the rest of the ride in silence. He put on some dark glasses so his eyes and his mood remained hidden.

Casey had never been good at small talk. Silence didn't disturb her. She watched the city as they drove along the waterfront, her artist's eyes picking out faces in the crowd, a certain cast of light on the water, a stone tower that would be perfect for sketching on slate-colored paper. She looked at the world with eyes that saw each color and put a name to it. Terracotta, burnt sienna, Payne gray, yellow ocher. The river was Van Dyke brown and the bridges spanning it were verdigris and gray, with brick red and Naples yellow showing in some stone buildings. Vermilion mopeds dashed up and down the cobblestone streets. Pedestrians in navy-blue coats hurried home through the dusk.

The car turned a corner and Tonio parked beneath an emerald-green and white-striped awning. "Here we are," he said.

Casey blinked and looked at her companion. His head was against the seat and he hadn't moved. "I think he's asleep," she whispered.

Tonio shook his head. "What an exciting date," he teased, but his voice, too, was soft.

"Maybe we should take him back home. Is he often tired like this after a practice?"

"Yes. He drives himself too hard. Exercise in the mornings, practices, meetings, photo sessions with the sponsors, more exercise and a tactics session with the team. He gets up at five thirty every morning."

"That's a long day," said Casey. She looked at her watch. Nine p.m. "Perhaps we should just let him sleep."

"He'll never forgive me." Tonio grinned. "Hey, Alex, wake up. You're going to miss your reservation." He reached over the seat and tapped Alessandro's shoulder.

"Leave me alone, Zazu," said Alessandro, then he sat up and took off his dark glasses. "Are we here already?" He rubbed his face and looked sheepish. "I'm sorry. Forgive me. Usually I don't fall asleep in the company of a lovely woman."

"Usually your dates chatter like parrots, keeping you awake," Tonio said. "At least this one is quiet. Very restful, if you ask me."

"I didn't," said Alessandro. "Now, act like a real chauffeur and open the door for Casey. You'll have to excuse him," he told her. "I have to tell him everything."

"Who is Zazu?" asked Casey. "Your girlfriend?"

"Zazu?" Alessandro laughed. "Zazu was a he, not a she. He was the trainer in the soccer school I went to when I was ten. He used to wake us up every morning at five a.m. for our first training session. I hated it, but it became a habit. Now I'm up every morning before dawn."

For some reason, Casey found she was relieved that Zazu wasn't one of Alessandro's girlfriends. "I wake up early too. I love the morning and everything is so peaceful. It's my favorite time of day."

Alessandro smiled. "I like it too, but sometimes I wish I could lie in bed and be lazy for a while."

* * * *

The restaurant was small, in the old section of town, and it looked very crowded. Casey's heart sank as every head swiveled around to stare at her as Alessandro took her elbow and steered her to her seat. There was a sudden hush then a flurry of agitated whispers. The headwaiter hurried over.

"Signor Sottini! We're so honored to have you here tonight. What can I get you to drink? Some champagne? Some wine?"

Alessandro started to speak then glanced at Casey. "What would you like?" he asked her.

The waiter looked surprised. Casey was grateful, though. "Right now, I'd just like some sparkling mineral water to drink, and with dinner, just a glass of red wine."

"Is that all?" the waiter cried. "And you, Signor Sottini, what can I get for you?"

"The same," said Alessandro. "What is your special tonight?"

"To start I have salmon tartar, or an omelet with caviar, or fresh asparagus with balsamic vinegar. For the main course, I have a stuffed turbot, grilled sole and a wonderful fresh crab with spinach and cheese. Would you care to see the menu?"

"What would you like?" Alessandro asked Casey.

"The asparagus sounds lovely and so does the grilled sole."

"That's perfect. I'll have the same." Alessandro nodded.

"Fine, fine." The man hurried away, snapping his fingers at one of the waiters. "Carlos, a bottle of red house wine for Signor Sottini!"

Casey raised her eyebrows. "Wow! Now that's service."

"There are some compensations to fame," said Alessandro, with a smirk.

The asparagus arrived within minutes. Casey tasted a spear and sighed. "This is wonderful. They mixed walnut oil with the balsamic vinegar... What a good idea."

"I suppose you don't eat as well in America," Alessandro said.

"It depends on where you are, but no, usually it's not as good."

"You can eat them with your fingers," he said, picking one up and nibbling on it.

"I didn't know that," she admitted. "Are you sure?"

"One of my ex-fiancées was a society girl. She tried to civilize me. Some things stuck." He made a sour face. "And some things didn't. I suppose you think most soccer players are barbarians too?"

"No," she answered. "I've never met any soccer players except you and I don't know you at all. How could I judge you?"

"I don't mean... Forgive me. I'm not usually so rude. So...how do you like Italy so far?" His grin was boyish now. His face was mobile and expressive, and when he looked at her, he gave her his whole attention. Casey had never been with someone so vibrant.

"I love Italy," she ventured, "The people are all so kind. I wasn't sure what I was getting into, but I don't regret it." She picked up another asparagus spear and ate it. As she did, she noticed the people at the table next to them staring at her. She frowned then noticed that everyone in the restaurant seemed to be focused on them. She turned to Alessandro and whispered, "I feel like I'm in a fishbowl."

"It will wear off in a few minutes. I'm so used to it, I'm sorry I didn't think to warn you." He ate his asparagus and looked at Casey's plate. "Aren't you going to eat that last one?" He eyed it hopefully.

Casey laughed. "You can have it." She watched as he reached over for it, eating with obvious relish, then took another glance around and saw that the crowd had shifted its interest away from them. She felt her shoulders relax. When she turned her attention back to him, Alessandro was using the silver fingerbowl. There was a slice of lemon in it.

"I once heard about someone mistaking this for soup at a dinner party," he said, drying his hands. "Supposedly when that happens, the hostess has to pretend its soup too. Do you think that's true?"

Casey rinsed her fingers, swirling them in the warm water. Immediately a waiter came with fresh napkins and took the bowls away. "I don't know," she admitted. "I was never at a place fancy enough for fingerbowls." She leaned forward. "As a matter of fact, before you used it, I thought it was soup."

He looked startled then laughed. "You're kidding."

Casey sat back in her chair and gave a mischievous grin. "You almost believed me."

"I did, didn't I?" He shook his head. "You make me laugh. No, I didn't mean it like that." His tone became more serious. "I haven't had so much fun with a woman in ages. Ever." He glanced up at her, his eyes bright. "You didn't tell me why you came to Italy. Was it to work? I know you're not a journalist, so what brought you here? Not that I'm complaining."

"I won a contest and first prize was a scholarship to an art school here. I was thrilled and I needed to get away from my memories. It seemed the right thing to do at the time," Casey said, smoothing the tablecloth with her hand.

"I'm sorry about your husband," he said. "It must have been very difficult for you."

"It was."

"How did he die?"

"In a car crash. A horrible, banal accident. He skidded on ice, lost control of his car and crashed into a tree. He was killed instantly." Casey stared at her plate. "That's all I want to say, if you don't mind."

"No, I don't mind." He reached over the table and took her hand. After a moment's pause, he changed the subject. "Have you been anywhere else in Italy? Have you been to Venice or Verona or Siena?"

The murmur of the crowd rose and fell around them, but Casey was conscious only of Alessandro's warm voice and the feel of his hands covering hers. "No, I haven't had time," she said. When he touched her, her thoughts scattered.

"I would love to take you to Florence. There are some incredible art museums there. You would adore it. In Siena, in the old village, there is a famous horse race once a year. The horses are ridden bareback and the whole countryside is decked out in colorful silks. The race is next weekend and I have no game, for once. We could go, if you'd like."

Casey stared at her hand entwined with his. Tightness in her throat was making it hard to speak. "I don't know," she whispered finally. She was afraid to look at him. His eyes were too magnetic—they stared straight into her, piercing the protective walls she'd built around her heart. She hadn't had any romantic thoughts at all since her husband had died. She hadn't been the slightest bit interested. But Alessandro stirred something within her and she wasn't sure if she was ready.

"Please?" he said. His voice was very soft. His hand, holding hers, trembled.

"Who ordered the crab?" a waiter shouted, holding a plate high over his head as he weaved through the restaurant.

Casey gasped, startled.

"I'm not letting you go," said Alessandro, leaning forward. "I won't."

Casey looked at him. Her heart was thumping so hard her chest shook with each beat. "I don't want you to," she said. A prickle ran up and down her arms. A breeze could have picked her up and carried her away. For the first time since David had died, there was a spark of warmth in her heart. She wanted to laugh aloud, or weep. She wasn't sure which, but it was a feeling of being alive and she reveled in it.

"Your cheeks are glowing," he told her.

"It's because of you," she said. "I think..." She blushed even harder.

"Yes?" His grin was infectious and Casey found herself grinning too.

"I think I like you, Alessandro Sottini, and I'm glad you decided to give me a second chance for the interview."

"Oh." His face fell. "The interview. I forgot all about that." He looked at her, but his eyes no longer held their spark of fun. "Is that the only reason you came to dinner tonight?"

"I have to admit it was," said Casey. She sighed and tilted her head. "I'm sorry if I hurt your feelings. The only reason I came to dinner was to interview you. But I'm finding more reasons to stay," she told him.

He gave her a brilliant smile. "Really?"

"Do you need to ask?" Casey peered at him. "No, don't answer that question. I'm sorry. It's just that you put me off balance. I didn't expect you to be…well, as you are," she finished with a shrug.

Alessandro stared at her with his uncanny amber eyes. His lashes made spiky shadows on his high cheekbones. He didn't smile. Instead, he reached across the table again and took her other hand. "When I touch you, I feel something I've never felt before," he said almost to himself. "When I saw you, my heart nearly stopped beating. I've never had to beg a woman to go out with me—usually they are throwing themselves at my feet. But I was ready to beg for you."

"Does it amuse you to have women at your feet?" Casey asked, feeling a little stab of jealousy.

"No, I can't say that I appreciate it. I have a hard time accepting that most women only love me because I'm a handsome soccer star. I won't base a relationship on those two things. I won't be handsome for the rest of my life and a soccer career is a pitifully short thing. What will happen when I'm retired and getting gray hair? Most women can't see past the outside and it annoys me." He was mercurial, his expressions and moods reflecting in his eyes. Now he was serious again, his face somber as he gazed at her.

"It would bother me as well," said Casey. She pulled her hand away and tried to gather her thoughts. It seemed as though he was waiting for her to say something, but she didn't know what.

"You tend to avoid the point," said Alessandro.

"I'm sorry, was there a point?" Casey looked at him, feeling cornered. *How have I gotten into this?*

"Yes, definitely. I want to know if you are interested in me as a man, or simply the soccer player for your article."

"I don't know you well enough," said Casey. "Are all you Italians so direct?"

"Yes." Alessandro nodded, his face grave. "We know what we want and when we find it, we don't waste time."

Casey took a sip of her water then set down the glass. "All right. You were honest with me, so I'll be straight with you."

"So American. I love it," said Alessandro before he flashed his pearly whites. He reached across the table and took her hands in his.

"You unbalance me and make me feel how inexperienced I am." Casey stopped, uncertain how to proceed.

He seemed startled then flushed. "I'm sorry. I never wanted to make you uncomfortable. That wasn't my intention."

"I know." Casey looked at their hands, still entwined on the tabletop. She could feel his pulse beating in his wrist and his fingers tightened on hers, tickling her palm. "I don't know if I'm ready for a relationship with anyone. I'm still feeling incredibly fragile. Perhaps I was only trying to get away from my past when I came here. I don't know. I'm trying to get my life in order and it's proving harder than I thought it would be."

"Why?" he asked.

"My husband's family is possessive of me. They were my foster parents, actually, and I married their only son."

His hands tightened on hers. "You must be close to them."

Casey sighed. "I am, but I'm all they have left…and since David died, they hardly let me out of their sight. It was a struggle just to get away. For the first time, I'm independent of them, but at the same time, it makes me feel incredibly guilty. I just don't know what to do."

"Let me help you," he said, his voice gentle.

"How?" She was close to tears now. His voice was so tender and his hands so warm. "Do you really want to?"

"I do." He leaned over the table toward her.

"Here's the sole!" cried the waiter, whipping their empty plates away and sliding two steaming fish beneath their noses.

"*Grazie*, Paolo," sighed Alessandro, glaring in mock exasperation at the waiter.

"My pleasure," he answered, bowing and flipping his hand. "Enjoy your meal!"

Casey took a bite of her meal and laughed at his expression. "Eat your fish before it gets cold. It tastes wonderful," she said.

He raised one eyebrow. "It does look good. Casey, will you answer my question? Will you let me become part of your life?"

She stared at her grilled sole and it seemed to stare back at her. 'Just say yes!' she could almost hear it say. She looked back up at Alessandro. He was still leaning forward, still waiting for an answer. "Yes," she whispered. She cleared her throat. "Yes, I'd like that very much," she said in a stronger voice.

Alessandro grinned. "Very well, I will start tomorrow. At ten a.m., you will come to the stadium to watch the practice. If you like," he added, raising his eyebrows.

"I'd like that," she said.

"Then we will go out for a picnic lunch in the country. This weekend we will go to Siena and see the Palio, the famous horse race I told you about. I will reserve two rooms in a beautiful hotel."

Casey put her hand on his mouth. "Enough planning. I said you could be part of my life, I meant that I'd like to get to know you better. It didn't mean you could boss me around. I don't need an army general, I need a...a..." She hesitated.

"A boyfriend? A lover?" Alessandro asked innocently, flashing a charming smile.

"A friend," replied Casey, biting her lip to keep from laughing.

"Okay, we take it one day at a time," he agreed.

Casey stared at him. "Are you serious?"

"Yes, aren't you?" He raised his eyebrows. "I thought I was being practical for once, looking ahead to the future. Usually I don't see past the next soccer season."

"How far ahead were you looking?" she asked.

"Further than I've ever seen," he murmured. He didn't elaborate and they ate their sole in companionable silence.

Dessert was fresh raspberries and homemade ice cream. Casey finished and leaned back, sated. "That was perfectly wonderful," she told Alessandro.

"Thank you. I like this place very much. The crowd is very considerate, so no one runs over and begs for an autograph. Actually, most of the people here already have my autograph, so they don't bother me anymore." He grinned.

They stared at each other, Casey's heart thumping. It was so strange how she reacted to his presence. He only had to look at her with his magnificent eyes and her pulse quickened. He reached out and stroked her cheek.

At that instant, a flash blinded her.

"Hey...!" Casey cried, spinning around.

A photographer sprinted out of the doorway. Alessandro had leaped to his feet, but was too late to do anything.

"I'm sorry, that's what usually happens when women go out with me." His voice was apologetic. "I hope this won't change anything," he said, his expression worried.

"I don't know," Casey said, getting to her feet. She wondered if she should be upset about the photographer but decided she was too exhausted even to think about it. "Can we leave now? I'm a bit tired and I have to write an article and email it before tomorrow morning."

"What will you write? You didn't ask me any questions."

"I went to the library and studied your club's magazine. Don't worry, it will be very flattering and I won't give away all your deep, dark secrets."

"Ha ha, very funny. I didn't tell you anything too deep and dark. Or at least I hope I didn't."

"No, but I know what I'm going to write."

* * * *

Alessandro held the car door open then slid in next to her. Tonio pulled into the street and Alessandro leaned back and put his arm around Casey. She didn't pull away. He didn't try to hold her. He just let her rest her head on his shoulder. She sighed and snuggled closer.

"So, ask me now," he whispered into her ear. "Ask me anything."

"What time shall I be ready tomorrow?"

He chuckled. "Ten sharp."

"And how nice is the hotel in Siena?"

"It's incredible. You'll love it. You can have your own room and I'll be right next door, in case you need anything in the middle of the night." His voice was warm and tickled her neck.

"And then we take it day by day," she said with a yawn.

"Sounds good to me," he answered, his voice just a murmur in her ear.

By the time Tonio arrived on Casey's street, they were asleep in each other's arms, her head resting on his shoulder, his cheek pressed against her hair.

Tonio scratched his head and grinned. "This must have been a fascinating conversation," he said, as he tapped Alessandro on the arm.

"Zazu, let me sleep just five minutes more," muttered Alessandro.

"Fine, have it your way." Tonio woke Casey and helped her out of the car.

"Shh, he's sleeping," he said, pointing to the soccer player slumped in the back seat.

"I was too," she admitted, shaking her head to clear it. "You drive too well for an Italian," she added.

"No, I drive perfectly for a romantic Italian. Good night, Miss, I'll be by to pick you up at ten."

"Thank you, Tonio," she said as he drove away.

On the stoop, sitting in a rocking chair, was her neighbor, Signora Maldono, a delicate piece of crochet on her lap. "How was dinner?" the woman asked with a large wink.

Casey smiled. She was used to her neighbors asking her about her life. "Great. We went to the Pescatorii and I had the most wonderful asparagus and sole. You'll have to go someday. It's quite lovely."

"I've heard of it, of course! It's one of the best-known places in Italy, my dear. Your date didn't just take you to dinner, he took you for a celebration of gastronomy."

Casey waved then walked up the three flights of stairs to her apartment. She was yawning, but she had to write and email an article to Greta before she could sleep.

After pouring herself a cup of ice water, she sat at her desk and jotted down some ideas. Then she turned on the computer and wrote an interview, using most of the information she'd gotten at the library. She checked her notes then emailed everything to Greta, apologizing for what she knew was a total disaster but adding an address where she could reach Alessandro's press agent for photos.

"I didn't get any of Ilario's questions answered, either," muttered Casey as she hit Send. "As a journalist, I'm a total loss."

She turned off the computer and the light then stood in the darkness a minute, trying to sort out her churning emotions. When she closed her eyes, all she could see was Alessandro's smile.

Chapter Three

Casey hummed the last love song she'd heard on the radio that morning as she went down the stairs to the street. It was a bright, cool morning and there was a line outside the bakery. She joined the queue to get her almond croissants. As she stepped inside the shop, a sudden hush descended on the crowd. She glanced at the baker, Mr. Panello, a smile on her lips. It faded when she saw his awed expression.

He handed her a bag of warm croissants.

"Good morning," she faltered. "How are you today?"

"Fine," he said. "Did you see the morning paper?"

"No, should I?" She was worried. Had something happened in America? Why the strange stares?

"Here, look." He handed her the paper over the counter.

It was the *Daily News,* and on the front cover was a picture of Casey and Alessandro, hand in hand at the table in a position of tender intimacy. Splashed across the page was the headline *Soccer Star Sottini to Wed American!*

"I don't believe it." She put out her hand to steady herself on the counter.

"Congratulations," said an old woman, tapping Casey on the arm.

The older people and the men smiled and patted her fondly, but the young women glared at her with fierce expressions.

"It's not true," said Casey, trying to gather her thoughts. "I simply went to dinner. I hardly know the man…"

A young boy dashed up and waved a piece of paper at her. "Can you get me his autograph?" he shouted.

Casey recognized the boy as one of her neighbor's children. "I don't know," she said. But the boy looked so crestfallen she took his scrap of paper and said, "I'll try."

She wanted to give the newspaper back to the baker, but he winked and told her to keep it. She knew her cheeks must be bright red and she fumbled the coins as she counted the money for the croissants. "Thank you for the newspaper," she said, backing out of the shop. "Really, it's quite exaggerated, I assure you."

Waving and smiling, she turned and dashed to her apartment before anyone else could stop her.

Once in the apartment, she shoved the newspaper under the couch and tossed the bag of croissants on the kitchen table. She glanced at her watch. It was almost eight. Casey plugged in the machine and she soon had a cup of freshly squeezed orange juice along with her coffee. Then she called Ilario, but he was out. She left a message, saying that she hadn't had time to ask the questions he'd wanted, but if he wished, he could call her back.

* * * *

Tonio, came to pick her up at ten sharp. "Are you a football fan?" he asked her.

She shook her head. "I've never seen a soccer game in real life."

"Well, then, what are we waiting for? Get in, get in!" cried Tonio, opening the door with a flourish.

They drove to the back gate of the stadium, where the guard recognized Tonio and waved them inside. He parked in an underground parking lot and accompanied Casey to an area in the stands where the invited guests of the Squadra di Torino watched the practice games.

"Alessandro is getting ready to play, as you can imagine," he told Casey. "But he'll be here as soon as he can. Perhaps he'll stop by on the way to the field. Why don't we sit here?"

There was a group of women and children a little ways away in a separate section of the stands. "Those are the players' wives and families," explained Tonio. "That woman over there with the little girl is English. Her husband is one of our offensive players. He's the number fifteen down on the field warming up. Perhaps you'd like me to introduce you? You must miss speaking in your native tongue."

"No, that's all right. I'm speaking English with you."

"It's not the same thing," said Tonio with a wide grin.

Casey looked toward the field and saw three players coming out of a doorway. "There's Alessandro," she said, her heart starting to thump hard. It was ridiculous, really. She was a grown woman, yet here she was, her cheeks flushed and her eyes as bright as stars.

Alessandro searched the crowd and when he saw Casey, his face broke into a huge grin. He waved and Casey waved back. At once, every head swiveled her way as people craned their necks to see who she was.

"Who is that man with Alessandro?" Casey asked Tonio, trying not to notice all the stares in her direction.

"That's the French player, Pierre Deslyons, and our goalie, the *Great* Fabricio."

"The *Great* Fabricio?" Casey asked. She raised her eyebrows. "It sounds like a name for a trapeze artist."

Tonio looked at her and said with mock severity, "Our goalie is one of the best in the world. He is not a circus star."

Casey grinned. "I was just teasing. I know how proud you Italians are of your soccer players."

He pointed to another player. "Keep an eye on that guy, he'll be playing against Alessandro for the practice. He's a new kid, from Argentina. He's amazing. He runs faster and kicks harder than any player I've ever seen."

Casey smiled at Tonio. "I have no idea what to expect. It's all new to me." She turned her attention back to the field, to watch as the players finished their warm-up run and stretches, and took their places for the practice.

A whistle blew and the assistant coach yelled, "Play!"

The practice match started at a slow pace with small passes as the players jogged to further warm up their muscles. The crowd shouted encouragement and cheered any time anyone kicked anywhere near a goal. Soon a game had begun in earnest, players forgetting that it was just a practice and giving it their all. Tonio explained the rules and soon Casey had a good grasp of the game. It wasn't as complicated as it had first seemed, especially with Tonio pointing out the different plays and fouls.

A tackle sent Alessandro crashing to the ground and the crowd drew its breath. They let out a collective sigh of relief when he got up and shook off the dirt on his shirt. Casey had grabbed the edge of her seat when he'd fallen and only relaxed when she saw he was unhurt. The game resumed, but now the referees held the players in check, whistling if one made contact with another.

When the practice was finished, the crowd applauded. The players waved and trotted back to their locker room. Alessandro passed close to Casey's seat and called to her.

"How did you like it?"

She leaned over the railing and grinned. "I didn't fall asleep, if that's what you meant."

"Ah, it was too short, that's why. If you come see a whole game, I'm sure you'll doze off."

"Especially if you're playing," she teased, flipping her hair back.

"So, you'll meet me downstairs?"

"What's wrong?" Casey wondered why his expression had clouded.

"Nothing. You'll wait, won't you? I have to take a shower." He glanced over her shoulder and grimaced. "I'd better be going."

He waved again and jogged to the locker room. Casey wondered why he'd left in such a hurry, but when a group of autograph-hunters pushed her aside, crying his name, she understood.

"Wow," said Casey, rubbing her foot where someone had stepped on it. "He sure is popular."

"You have no idea," said Tonio, shaking his head.

Most people's attention turned to Casey.

"Hey, I recognize you!" cried a voice from the group.

"It's Alessandro's fiancée!" said someone else.

Casey found herself besieged on all sides, as everyone wanted to know who she was and if it was true she was marrying Alessandro. Most people started asking for her autograph, while one woman shoved the morning paper in her face.

Casey frowned. Her Italian was still sketchy, but she managed to wave the woman away.

Tonio made a barricade with his body, but it didn't help when another player came near and the autograph-hounds lunged toward the railing.

"I thought these seats were only for the players' guests," she muttered to Tonio, as another person pushed her aside.

"They are, but obviously there's been a mix-up," said Tonio. He elbowed his way through the crowd and took Casey to another section of the stands. He flashed his ID card, and the guard let them in. "This part is for the players' families. We'll be much more comfortable here."

"But, Tonio," Casey said, nervous, "you're not part of any player's family. And neither am I," she added.

"I don't want to argue that point." Tonio grinned. "This is Jane Leeds. Her husband is our English player, the number fifteen I pointed out to you before."

Casey saw a tall, blonde woman with a small girl on her lap. The child looked up at her with wide, blue eyes and gave a shy smile.

"Jane, this is Casey, she's from America," Tonio said.

"Hello." Jane smiled and shook Casey's hand. "Are you a friend of Tonio's? I'm so pleased to meet you. This is my little girl, Mandy."

"Hello, Jane, hi, Mandy. What pretty eyes you have!" Casey said, smiling at the little girl. "Actually I'm here to see Alessandro Sottini play," she told Jane.

"Ha!" interjected Tonio. "Don't you read the paper? This is Casey, Alessandro's new girlfriend."

Casey wished the chair he was sitting in would swallow him up. "I'm a journalist and I'm writing an article about Alessandro."

"Oh," said Jane, raising her eyebrows. "What are you doing in Torino?" she asked. Then she shook her head. "Oh, I forgot, you're a journalist. What magazine are you working for?"

Casey blushed. "*Watch Out!*, an American women's magazine, asked me to write an article about Alessandro. I'm here to study art for a year. I have an apartment overlooking the plaza, near the ruins."

"Art?" Jane nodded. "There's an excellent international art school here, of course." She noticed Casey's hand. "Are you married?" she asked, pointing to the wedding band Casey still wore.

Casey hesitated. "No, I'm a widow," she said. "What a pretty dress Mandy has," she went on, wanting to change the subject.

Jane's face had altered a bit when she'd said 'widow'. Now her brown eyes were full of sympathy. "That must be hard," she said. "I'm sure Alessandro will be a big help."

Casey's face grew hot. "Honestly, we're just friends," she said.

"Casey!" Alessandro grabbed her from behind, spun her around and kissed her on the lips. "Shall we go? I reserved lunch in a splendid restaurant. Hurry, we have to be there before one."

He checked his watch. "I'm afraid we're running behind and I don't want to be late," he said to Jane. "You can get to know Casey better another time."

Jane's eyebrows climbed higher. "Just friends?" she said with a wide grin.

Casey stuck her hand out. "It was so nice to meet you," she said, hoping her face was not as red as it felt.

"I'm sure we'll meet again," said Jane, smiling broadly. "Alessandro has never brought any of his girlfriends here before," she added sotto voce. "He must be madly in love. Congratulations, Casey."

"Come on!" cried Alessandro, taking her arm and tucking it in his.

It seemed to Casey that the whole crowd turned to watch them leave the stadium.

In the quiet and comfort of the car, Alessandro put his arm around Casey and held her close.

"I hope you enjoyed the game," he said to her. "It was just a practice, but maybe you got an idea of what soccer is all about. What did you think of it?"

"It was very interesting," said Casey. She tried to think of something else to say, but she was pretty sure her appreciation of watching him run around in shorts wasn't quite what he meant. "I was worried when you got knocked down. Does that happen a lot?"

"I'm afraid so." For the first time Alessandro looked grim. "It's not supposed to happen during a practice, but there is fierce competition between the first and second-string players. There are a few who are waiting for their chance to play."

"Don't you all take turns?" Casey asked.

"No, only the best play and we play until we drop," said Alessandro. His mouth twisted. "Don't listen to me, I'm just a bit tired today."

Casey stroked his arm. He turned to her and his face lost its hard edges. "So if only the best play, you must be in all the games, right?" she asked.

He smiled at her, his amber eyes suddenly tender. "Right," he said and his voice was like a caress. He leaned toward her and again her heart started thumping. Their lips touched in a butterfly brush, just a gentle and shy at first, then with more assurance. He probed softly with his tongue and her lips parted —

"Here we are!" Tonio announced, driving up to a huge stone edifice covered with climbing roses in all shades of pink and yellow. He got out and held the door open.

Alessandro drew back, his expression a mixture of yearning and resignation. "Yes, here we are," he echoed.

"Oh, it's a like fairy-tale castle," cried Casey, stepping out of the car and blinking in the strong sunlight.

"Actually, it once belonged to a prince," Alessandro said. "But he moved to the South of France and now it's a restaurant."

He turned to his chauffeur. "Tonio, will you pick us up at three? I have to be back at the stadium at four thirty, I have a meeting with the sponsors."

"Another photo session?" Tonio asked.

"No." Alessandro shrugged. "Something about the European Cup. C'mon, Casey. Follow me," he said with a sexy grin.

The dining room was done in tones of rose and ocher, with lots of gleaming woodwork. The multi-paned windows looked out over a terraced garden.

The menu, Alessandro explained, was limited to two entrées and two main courses, and changed every day. You could choose between antipasto and a pasta entrée, then between fish and fowl or a meat course. That day the choices included a fondue Savoyarde for two.

"What do you think?" Alessandro asked. "I know it's summer, and some people might think it's too hot for a fondue, but it might be fun."

"What is it? I've never had one," she added.

"They give you chunks of bread and you dip them in melted cheese. It's quite filling, so if we get it, we'll have to forgo anything else."

"Let's try it," said Casey. "I'm hungry and it's cool here in the dining room."

"All right, but I'm warning you. If you lose a piece of bread off your fork, you have to pay the price." His eyes were sparkling when he said that.

"What price?"

"I get to ask you to do something and you have to agree." Now he wriggled his eyebrows. "And you get to do the same for me."

The fondue was a small, enameled pot sitting on a hot plate. They each had a long fork and there was a pile of bread cut into small squares on a platter. Casey closed her eyes and inhaled the delicious fragrance coming from the bubbling cheese. It had a hint of white wine and garlic in it, and something else. Casey dipped her bread in the melted cheese and nibbled it, trying to guess what it was.

"Kirsch," said Alessandro, reading her mind. "It has kirsch in it. And we each have a little glass of it after we finish the fondue."

Casey pulled out her fork. "Where's my bread?" she cried, peering into the pot.

"Aha! Now you're in trouble. I'll have to think of something particularly horrible for you," said Alessandro, rubbing his hands together cheerfully. "Let's see, what shall it be? Hmmm. Let me think.

Something really awful." His eyes crinkled in mirth. "I know. You'll have to answer all my questions and tell me your deepest secrets. We'll start with where you grew up. I picture the United States as one huge metropolis, covered with skyscrapers and casinos, like Times Square or Las Vegas. Did you grow up in the city?"

"No, I grew up in a small town. To me Torino is a big city, although I did work for a while in Columbus, Ohio," Casey said.

"What did you do?"

"I was an illustrator for *Watch Out!* magazine. It was a lot of fun, but when I got married, I stopped. We moved back to the town I grew up in and we lived in a little cottage near a park."

"Did you work then too?"

"Of course, but I did mostly freelance work. When my husband died...I didn't do very well for about a year, then I pulled myself together and I entered a contest. The first prize was a year of art school in Italy. I won and here I am," Casey said. She ran her hand through her long hair, brushing it back from her face. "My life has changed so radically that sometimes I wonder if I'm still the same person."

Alessandro smiled. "You will always be the same."

Casey smiled back at him. "It's strange. I feel as if I've known you for years instead of only a couple days."

"That is because there is a spark between us," said Alessandro. "In Italy, we believe that you can fall in love in a second. Just one glance, just one touch, and you know that person is the right one." He gazed at her, his amber eyes intense.

Casey shrugged. "In America, we're a bit more circumspect. We think you should get to know a person before falling in love with them."

"If I fell in love with someone, I would want to get to know that person," Alessandro pointed out. "If someone doesn't interest me, why should I waste my time?"

"Touché," Casey said. "You should be a lawyer, not a soccer player."

Alessandro's expression grew more serious. "You're right. A lawyer is a more interesting profession — it lasts longer, is more useful to society and is something a woman would appreciate. A soccer player is an ephemeral beast. Here one day, gone the next. A few years at the top then the slow slide downward." He frowned. "The scary part is it could happen to me tomorrow. One serious injury and I could lose the ability to play."

Casey was surprised he was being so introspective. He hadn't seemed like the type. "Why even think of that?" she asked.

He raised his eyebrows and gave her a crooked grin. "Because, for the first time in my life, I find myself looking toward the future and I want to have something tangible to offer to the woman I love."

There was a small silence while Casey digested this. Then she smiled and said, "Whatever you decide to do, I'm sure it will be enough to offer. You have yourself, Alessandro, and I think that's all anyone could want."

"Thank you, Casey," said Alessandro. He cleared his throat, a pleased look on his face.

The waiter came and cleared the table, and asked if they wanted dessert.

"No thanks," said Casey. "I'd like a coffee, though."

"No dessert for me either. After the fondue, I'll have to fast for three days before being able to run again." Alessandro sighed. "Just coffee please," he told the waiter.

"What will you do when you retire?" Casey asked.

He shrugged then pointed out of the window at the extensive gardens. "What do you see out there?" he asked.

Casey looked at the view. The gardens were laid out in three levels, one very formal with trimmed boxwood hedges forming intricate designs and, in the middle, fruit-bearing trees pruned into round balls. The next level, down a wide flight of white marble stairs, had a fountain in the middle of an intricate herb garden. The last level was the flower garden, with white gravel paths winding through it. Casey said, "It's beautiful." She sipped her coffee, her eyes on Alessandro. He seemed to be hesitating. "What is it?" she asked.

"I love gardens," said Alessandro with a nod. "When I stop playing soccer, I'm planning to study to be a landscape artist." He said that almost as if he were embarrassed and, as he spoke, he peered at Casey's face. "Do you think that's strange?" he asked.

"No, of course not." She took his hand. "Let's go for a walk in the garden and you can tell me about it," she said.

Outside, they wandered past the clipped hedges, down the marble steps and walked around the fountain. Under the splashing fountain in the shape of a nymph holding a jar, goldfish swam among the water lilies in the dark green water. When they got to the flower garden, Alessandro said, "I was afraid to tell you I wanted to be a landscape artist."

"Why?"

He shrugged. "It's not very glamorous."

Casey didn't dare laugh—he looked so serious. Instead, she said, "I'm afraid glamor is not high on my priority list." She took his hand. "I know nothing of plants or flowers. I don't have a green thumb and all the roses in my garden back home looked as if they had some terrible disease. Nothing I did seemed to help them. I sprayed them with bug spray, I put fertilizer in their dirt, I even sang to them one day. I heard on the radio that plants love music, so I went outside and sang. You can imagine my embarrassment when I found out the neighbors were home that day—and in their yard."

"What happened?"

"They waited until I finished my song, then they stepped out from behind the hedge and clapped."

Alessandro grinned. "You can sing to the plants, I'll prune them. Between us, we'll have the most beautiful garden in Italy."

Casey gave a start. "That's a nice dream, but it's too far in the future for me, at least right now," she said.

"No, it's not a dream." Alessandro took her arm and turned her around, facing him. He kissed her on the lips, her chin and her temples. Then he just held her, his chin resting on her shoulder.

Casey stood still, her emotions in turmoil. Her heart hammered and she closed her eyes.

Alessandro sighed. "You feel the way I do," he said. "I can tell."

Casey nodded. There was no use hiding it. She couldn't understand why she would even try. When Alessandro had his arms around her, she realized she had found a part of herself she hadn't even known was missing until then. His embrace was so right. She raised her head and when his lips brushed hers, her knees trembled. "I thought this sort of thing only happened in romance books," she said, stepping back and tucking a stray lock of hair behind her ears.

He smiled at her, his eyes bright.

Hand in hand, they strolled across the gravel path toward the flower garden. A few other people were there. Most were tourists with cameras around their necks.

"I told you about myself, now tell me a little about your childhood," said Casey.

"Is this for your article?" teased Alessandro.

"No, I sent it off this morning. It wasn't very edifying, I'm afraid. I hope you don't mind," she said with a grin.

"That's good. I like boring articles about me." He drew her in his arms and kissed her again.

"About your childhood," said Casey, prodding him in the chest. She flushed and darted a glance at a couple standing nearby. "Stop kissing me like that, someone might take a picture!"

"Oh yeah?" He raised an eyebrow and leered at her.

She tried not to giggle. "And their film will burst into flames. Now, can we talk?"

He grinned. "All right. I'll be good now. I grew up in soccer school. I started playing when I was six and when I was nine, a coach came and persuaded my parents to let me go to a special school. It wasn't a hardship. My parents were farmers, so they thought I was getting something they could never offer me. I had an enjoyable time...mostly." He nuzzled her neck then cleared his throat. "Sorry. I'd better stop. There are too many people in the garden with us."

Casey shivered at his touch. "You were awfully young when you began to play professionally. It doesn't seem as if you had much time to be a kid."

"I know." He frowned. "It wasn't so much a psychological strain as it was a physical one. Physically, I think I should have had more time to grow. I have problems with my knees because of early stress on my joints. Luckily, they have held up so far."

"That's terrible! Do many soccer players have that problem?"

"More than you'd guess. They take painkillers to help them get through the season and I've seen players…" He broke off and was silent. "I don't know if I should say any more."

"I'm not a journalist," said Casey with a rueful laugh. "I'm not going to write anymore articles about soccer players."

"I would have liked to have seen that boring one you wrote before you sent it off." He laughed but appeared worried just the same. He glanced at his watch and sighed. "Tonio will be waiting for us."

"I'm sorry, I should have showed it to you. If you want, I can show it to you now. Can you come to my apartment?" Casey bit her lip. Would he think her too forward?

He gave a wistful smile. "I wish I could, but Tonio has to drop me off at the club. I have a meeting."

"Oh, that's right. Sorry." She peered at him. "Why the sad face?"

"I won't see you until Friday. You're still coming to Siena with me, aren't you?" Now he looked anxious.

"Of course! I wouldn't miss it."

"I'll have Tonio pick you up at two p.m. Will that be all right?"

"I'll be waiting."

"Wonderful!" He pulled her behind a large boxwood hedge then hesitated before lowering his face to hers and kissing her on the lips. Casey wrapped her arms around his neck and pulled him closer. Now that they were out of sight, she opened her mouth to his and deepened her kiss. Her teeth clicked against his, then his tongue was tracing the edge of her lower lip. Her heart sped up and she pressed even closer, her own tongue slipping into his mouth. She moaned as he plunged his into her mouth, harder now, in a rhythm that left no doubts as to its significance. She could hardly breathe. There was a rush of heat between her legs, and when she moved against Alessandro, the hard ridge of his erection pressed into her belly.

He uttered a groan and drew back, resting his forehead on her shoulder. He was shaking. "Any more of this and I'll have you flat on your back right here on the grass," he said, his voice raw.

Casey's tightened her arms around him. "At least you stopped. I was about to let you push me over." She gave a shaky laugh. "Maybe we better go to the car."

"All right, but give me a minute." Alessandro tried to grin but it was strained. "I have to wait until, um, things have calmed down a bit." He reached over and smoothed her hair. "Although when you're near me, calm isn't how I'd describe myself."

Once in the car, Casey settled into his arms and was silent, watching the landscape roll by. She had stopped trying to analyze her feelings. She'd decided to take advantage of the opportunity life had so generously given her. Alessandro said he was falling in love with her, and something deep in her heart stirred. This weekend in Siena, she would find out if Alessandro was the one for her and if they had any kind of future together.

* * * *

Back at her apartment, she watered her plants and made herself a cup of tea. The late afternoon sun slanted into the window and colored the walls orange. When it set, dipping below the rooftops and cooling the air, Casey lay on her bed and thought of Alessandro.

She remembered his mahogany hair, cut short around his well-shaped head. She wondered what it would feel like to run her fingers through it. His eyes were light brown, like honey, and his lips were full and sensual. She loved how he spoke English with a spicy, Italian accent. In the soccer stadium, he had attracted everyone's attention. He was so at ease in front of the crowd and yet, with her, he could be so unsure. He was a mixture of self-assurance and introversion, and the combination was seductive.

She tried to imagine Alessandro at her house in Westerville, Ohio. She pictured him sitting on the porch, perched in the swing. He swayed back and forth. It was summer and the fireflies were starting to blink as they floated in the ultramarine air. Honeysuckle clambered up the porch railing and spilled in an exuberant, fragrant tangle down one side. She walked toward him.

Then the screen door to the kitchen opened and her husband walked out. The two men stared at each other.

Casey sat up with a start. She'd dozed off. Her tea was cold and night had fallen. Now the city lights were lit and downstairs, in the little café across the street, music was playing from the jukebox. She got up and closed her window, then she took a shower. All the while she tried not to think about David and about starting a new relationship, although she knew she'd have to face it soon.

Why did she feel guilty for going out with Alessandro?

Lying in bed again, she closed her eyes and tried to think of anything else, but David's gentle face kept appearing.

"Let me go," she whispered into the dark. "I'm sorry, but I don't want to mourn for you all my life."

"How can you forget me?" he asked her, pain in his blue eyes.

"I'll never forget you." Casey reached for him, but it was like reaching for smoke. "I'm trying to start over. If you were still alive, we would still be happy. But you're not and I'm so unhappy, David. I need someone in my life. I didn't realize how lonely I was until I met Alessandro."

"I'm sorry," David said. His voice was fading.

"I'm sorry too… I will always regret not being able to spend the rest of my life with you. I'll always feel cheated. But now I have to let you go."

Casey waited for a reply, but there was just the sound of traffic as cars drove by. Someone laughed on the street and the music still played, only now it was an Italian love ballad.

She got out of bed and wandered to the window. She parted the gauzy curtains and looked outside. The street was busy at night. There were three restaurants, a café, the bakery stayed open until late and there was even a used shoe store — open until well past midnight. All the shoes were the same price and there were some high-fashion shoes with nary a scratch on their supple leather.

Her chin cupped in her hands, Casey watched the people walking in the street. Italy was perfect for her. The sounds, the colors, the people, it all seemed right, somehow. She also knew she was relieved to be away from her in-laws. Sam and Ellen had meant well, but they had smothered her. Even now, hardly a day went by that she didn't get an email or a letter from them, begging her to take care and hurry home.

Home. Casey lay back on her bed and closed her eyes. Home was here, in Italy. With Alessandro—for as long as he wanted her. She shivered. Was she falling in love?

In the dark, she ran her hands over her own body. It had been too long since she'd had a lover. Now, when she thought of Alessandro, there was an ache between her thighs. She dipped her hand lower, delved into her silky pubic hair and found the sensitive nub of her clit with her fingertip. Sighing, she drew small circles around it, teasing herself. Moisture gathered and her finger moved faster, slipping over the swelling flesh. Her nipples tingled, and her other hand strayed to her breast and she took her nipple between her thumb and her forefinger, pinching it gently and tugging on it. She wished it were Alessandro's mouth on her breast and she arched her back, imagining him lying next to her, his hand between her legs, his thighs pressing against hers. She groaned and pulled harder on her nipple, imagined him taking it in his mouth and sucking hard, teasing it with the tip of this tongue.

She tried to picture him naked, with his sexy, bedroom eyes and his lithe, muscular body. She wondered how his cock looked and what size it was. A small moan escaped her lips. Throbbing sensations flooded her belly and she opened her legs wide. She slipped a finger into her cunt, feeling the slippery need that now made her breath come in quick gasps. She dug her heels into the covers, arching her buttocks off the bed, using two fingers now. It wasn't enough.

Panting, she raised her knees and pushed her fingers deeper, seeking release. She found her clit with her thumb and stroked. With her free hand, she grabbed a breast, then the other, rubbing her palm firmly over her sensitive nipples. Her nipples tingled and grew harder and her whole body strained toward deliverance. Her heart hammered, her breath came in gasps and a gush of warmth flooded her hand. Panting, she stroked herself to orgasm, but the pulsing release only accentuated her need. Visions of Alessandro, naked and in her bed, assailed her. Another climax shook her as she clutched at her throbbing cunt.

Spent, she rolled over and buried her head in the pillow. She hoped and prayed the weekend would bring the answers she sought.

Chapter Four

Casey looked in her purse and grimaced. Just enough for a sandwich at the café, then she had to go to the apartment and pack. Her art supplies were putting a dent in her budget.

In the café, the light was dim and it was cool. Casey smiled at the waiter who had dashed over to serve her. "I'd like a smoked ham sandwich and mineral water, please," she said.

"Right away!" He hesitated then blurted, "Are you really engaged to Alessandro Sottini?"

Casey wondered if she could collect a few lire for every person who asked her that. Her bank account would probably explode. She gave him a small smile and the answer she'd perfected by now. "We're not engaged. I hardly know him."

"Oh." He appeared to be disappointed. "Can you get me his autograph?" he asked.

He looked so eager that Casey laughed. "I'll have him fill up a notebook and I'll give them out. All right?"

She didn't think anything of the conversation, but soon she heard whispers from a nearby table, and when she glanced around, everyone seemed to be staring at her. Some looks were downright angry.

Casey frowned and wondered what she'd done. Alessandro must have been engaged to a hundred girls, from what the articles about him said. It must be her imagination, she decided.

The waiter brought her the sandwich and a bottle of fizzy mineral water. Casey ate, then, still conscious of the stares in her direction, hurried to pay her bill and go back to her apartment.

After a quick shower, she put on a pair of white cotton jeans and a yellow knit halter top. She twisted her hair into a chignon, fastening it with a gold clip. Then she packed the rest of her clothes into a small suitcase and at the stroke of two, Tonio rang her doorbell.

"Here, let me get that," he said, gallantly stooping and picking up her bag. "Where is the rest of your luggage?"

"That's it," said Casey.

He looked stunned. "That's it? Just one bag?" He grinned. "Are you sure you're a female? Whenever Alessandro took a woman anywhere, she most often had a load of..." He broke off and turned red. "I'm sorry, that was not, how do you say...diplomatic, was it? Can I start over again?"

Casey narrowed her eyes. "That's all right. I'll get over it."

"I'm not driving you to Siena, you know. We're to meet Alessandro in front of my apartment. He's trying to be discreet."

"Discreet?"

"He doesn't want anyone to know he's taking you to Siena." He waved his hands in a wide, Italian gesture. "Imagine. Women are all over him. He goes out in public with one, all the others have a fit." He made a face when he saw Casey's expression. "I don't think I explained that very well. Forget what I said."

Casey tried to smile, failed and shrugged. "Let's go."

In the car, Tonio tried to make small talk, but Casey wasn't in the mood. She was wondering if she was doing the right thing. The remarks about Alessandro's other women had rattled her. She hardly knew the man and now she was about to spend a whole weekend with him. And yet she knew she wanted him. The thought provoked a little shiver of nervous laughter.

Tonio lived in a residential part of the city, not far from Alessandro's apartment. As they drove up, Alessandro stepped out from a shadowed doorway. By the time Tonio had stopped the car, three people had already rushed up to Alessandro and demanded autographs. One girl insisted on kissing his cheek and when she got a glimpse of Casey sitting in the car waiting, she gave her a furious glare and stalked off.

Alessandro slid into the driver's seat and reached over to touch Casey's cheek in a light caress. "Sorry about all this... Shall we go?" He waved to Tonio and they set off, weaving in and out of the traffic.

The trip was amazing. After they left the city, the road wound through beautiful countryside. Alessandro drove well—maybe too fast for Casey's taste, but then again, everyone in Italy drove too fast for her taste.

The hotel was on a quiet street and their view overlooked an old park. Tall trees cast deep shade over the winding paths and stone benches. Casey's room was spacious and airy with windows covered with lace curtains. The walls were cream-colored and her bedspread was butter-yellow cotton piqué. A bouquet of white roses spread their perfume from the bedside table. An antique, full-length oval mirror hung on the wall and there was a comfortable armchair next to the bed.

She peeked into her bathroom and saw it was huge. It had a claw-foot tub, a very modern glassed-in shower, and the whole floor was covered with octagonal Italian terracotta tiles. The walls were cream and the towels were an orange plush. Another bouquet, this time of yellow roses, was perched on the windowsill, and in the far corner, an antique linen curtain hid the toilet from view.

"What a gorgeous place!" she cried, leaning over to smell the fragrant roses near her bed.

"It matches your yellow blouse," teased Alessandro. "Come look at my room!"

Casey raised her head from the roses and gave a mock pout. "I just got here!"

"It's right next door." He paused and gave a wicked grin. "I promise—I won't lock the door."

Alessandro's room was adjacent to Casey's—a door led from his to hers. It was smaller, with red floral wallpaper. On his bed was a velvet bedspread the color of port wine and there was a small fireplace. A bouquet of multicolored freesias was on the bedside table.

"When does the horse race start?" Casey asked.

"Tomorrow. Shall we stroll around the city, Cassandra?"

"Sounds lovely, Alex." She couldn't stop smiling. The rooms were opulent, the hotel was luxurious, and

Alessandro held her hand as if he never wanted to let her go.

It was wonderful and romantic walking along the small, winding streets. Alessandro pointed out the various sights for her. Then they wandered into the busier section of the city and he was recognized. A growing crowd of fans surrounded them and they ducked into an antique shop to escape them. The owner let them out through the back door, after getting an autograph from Alessandro, and they dashed to the hotel.

Now they were virtually prisoners in their own rooms. Casey looked at Alessandro. "What can we do?"

"Would you like to go to the Duomo and visit the museum?"

"Sounds great—shall we disguise ourselves?" Casey glanced out of the window where a crowd of people milled by the front door. In the streets, a constant stream of sightseers walked by, touring the beautiful city. "I don't think those people are going to get tired of waiting for you. Maybe you can wear one of my dresses and a big hat. We'll give them the slip!"

"You've been watching too much television," said Alessandro without a smile. "If you don't mind, I'll stay here and rest. You go ahead. I've already been to this museum anyway."

"Have you?" Casey said. She remembered Tonio's words. "Have you been here before as well?"

"Yes, I love this hotel," said Alessandro. He looked at her and cocked an eyebrow. "Why do you ask?"

"Were you here with another woman?" Casey tried to keep her voice light.

He leaned back in the armchair and folded his arms across his chest. "Actually, yes, I did come here with another woman. I never said I was a monk."

"No, you never did." Casey paused. "I don't mind. No, that's a lie," she said, shaking her head. "I do mind, terribly, but I'm not jealous. I think that everyone has the right to his past. As long as the present belongs to me," she added with a smirk.

"I agree. I'm terribly jealous about your husband — you married him and you loved him. But now I'm with you, so if anything, I feel fortunate," said Alessandro.

"I never dated anyone but him. So I'm not sure what I should act like," Casey said. "I'm afraid I'm not very interesting and you'll soon get tired of me."

"No, I don't think so. You aren't like any of the women I've dated before." He grinned faintly. "They were not very interesting, actually. Tonio couldn't stand any of them."

"You've never been in love before?" Casey asked, sitting on his lap.

"I guess not." He tilted his head. "You know, I don't think I ever thought about it before. We Italians are a romantic bunch. We like to believe we live and breathe love. It's not easy to admit when you're an Italian that you've never been in love."

"I suppose it's easier than admitting you don't like pasta," said Casey.

"If you don't like pasta, you're not an Italian." He ran his hands up her sides. "You'd better go, the museum won't stay open much longer."

"I'm gone. Are you sure you'll be okay?"

"I'll get some rest. It will do me good." He pulled her close and gave her a hug. "Go on, I'll still be here when you return."

"I know." She shivered as his hands caressed her back. "It's just that when you hold me, I'm not sure I want you to let me go," she whispered.

"I'm not sure, either. You'll have to go right now, or I won't be responsible for my actions."

"Liar," said Casey. "You strike me as being highly responsible." She pressed closer to him and his body branded on hers. His arms, wrapped around her shoulders, tightened. His thighs brushed her, and she could feel his arousal through the thin cotton of her jeans.

"You have exactly five seconds to get out of here," he murmured in her ear, his voice thick with desire.

"All right! I'm going. But only because you made me." Casey pulled back with regret.

"I don't want to rush you," said Alessandro.

"Or rush into anything," said Casey, kissing him as she got off his lap.

"No, I didn't say that. Go on now and be careful."

"I wish you would come with me."

"No, the crowds won't leave us alone. You'll have a better time without me."

Casey bit her lip but nodded. He was right. The people milling outside the hotel would never let him go by. The price of fame was getting steeper all the time, she decided as she left the room, closing the door softly behind her.

There was nobody in the hallways. The hotel doorman kept everyone away, but once she was on the street, someone must have recognized her and a murmur swept through the gathering. Casey hoped it was just her imagination, but it seemed to her a malevolent sound. Once past the doorway and the people, she picked up her pace, but not before a woman snatched at her arm and hissed, "Leave Alessandro alone!"

Another woman picked up the phrase and before Casey could duck around the corner, it had grown almost to a chant.

Shuddering, she ran down the street, heedless of where she went. When she was out of breath, she stopped and found herself in a narrow alley. Overhead, laundry flapped off taut clotheslines and red geraniums dotted every windowsill. A gray cat stood up and stretched before slinking off into the shadows. Above her head, a window opened and closed and a woman shouted at someone. There was music playing from a radio somewhere and the low roar of traffic.

Still nervous, Casey went to the mouth of the alley and peeked out. No one had followed her. The street was full of puttering buses, taxis honking their horns and trams clacking on their silver tracks. Overhead, electric lines crisscrossed like black spiders' webs. Tourists with cameras hanging from their necks gawked at the sights, while the natives scooted around on colorful Vespas. But there were no more cries of "Leave Alessandro alone!" Her shoulders slumped in relief.

Just across the way, Casey caught sight of the Duomo's black-and-white-striped tower. At least she wasn't lost. She wanted to return to the hotel, but the thought of facing the crowd again daunted her.

She stood for a while in the alley, undecided, then, taking a deep breath, strolled into the street. Nobody took any notice of her. Relieved, she walked to the museum and joined a crowd of American tourists. Blending into the group, she spent an hour looking at the exhibits and following a tour guide.

After that, she walked through the beautiful streets back to the hotel. The crowd was still there. She ducked her head and followed on the heels of a small group of people hurrying down the sidewalk. At the last minute, she elbowed her way firmly through, blurted her name to the harassed doorman and was let into the revolving doors. Angry shouts accompanied her.

A man leaning against the front desk talking to the concierge straightened when he saw her and said, "Casey!"

Her head snapped around and she saw who it was. "Ilario. How are you? Did you get my message?"

"I did, thank you." He waved at the doorway. "Fine crowd you drew."

She grimaced. "I don't think it's very funny."

"Neither do the hotel personnel. They called the police a few minutes ago. They'll clear everyone away. Then you can come and go as you please." Ilario took her by the elbow and led her toward the bar. "Come on, I'll buy you a drink. You look pale. Are you all right?"

"I'm fine, a bit stunned. I was getting used to the crowd at the stadium. Now I find out that Alessandro has a fan club in every city," Casey said with a wry laugh.

"Poor Casey." Ilario shook his head. "I could have warned you. I wish I had," he added. "Then perhaps you'd have gone out with me. It's not too late, is it? According to the morning paper, you and Alessandro have already set a date for your wedding." He pulled out a chair for her.

Casey sank into the chair and gaped at him. "That is not true," she sputtered. "We're just good —"

Casey Come Home

"Friends," Ilario finished for her, laughing. He sat down and brushed some imaginary crumbs off the table. "Are you staying in separate rooms?"

"I have the right to remain silent," said Casey, raising her hand.

"I might have known." Ilario sighed. "It's no use trying to interview a fellow journalist. We give nothing away, do we?"

"Technically, I'm not a journalist," Casey said. "I was just doing a favor for a woman I used to work with."

"Do you regret it?"

She looked at him. "No," she said with a crooked smile. "At least, not yet."

He nodded. "Then you'll have to get used to the press, the fans, the crowds and the inconvenience…at least until he stops playing. Then you'll see that the sunburst of fame fizzles out as quickly as it ignites. Perhaps that thought will put a damper on your enthusiasm for your soccer star?"

"I'm not worried about that." Casey glared at him. "I worry that someone I know will see the headlines and believe them. I'm worried that it will hurt my family, far-fetched as it may seem. But mostly I'm worried about Alessandro. He looks out the window and his shoulders slump. He appreciates his fans at the soccer games, but he wishes they would leave his private life alone. After all, they only love him because he plays soccer so well."

"How philosophical," said Ilario. "Can I quote you?"

"Are you writing an article about us?" Casey sat up straighter.

"No, relax. Waiter! Two pressed oranges." He shook his head. "I'm your friend, remember?"

"I'm sorry. I'm a bit on edge. Thank you for the library card. It was helpful. I found the magazines you mentioned and the interview went better than I could have hoped."

"Obviously," remarked Ilario, his eyebrow raised.

"Oh, ha. Very funny."

The waiter set two glasses of what looked like tomato juice in front of them, along with a silver sugar dish and a small crystal pitcher of ice water.

"What's this?" Casey asked.

"Freshly squeezed sanguine orange juice. Try it, it's delicious. You can add sugar or water if you find it's too strong."

Casey sipped her juice, made a face and added a spoonful of sugar and topped the glass up with water.

"You drink it just like an Italian," Ilario approved. "Ah, here comes your good friend."

She turned and waved to Alessandro. "I'd like to introduce you to Ilario de Baldini," Casey said.

"We've met." He shook Ilario's hand and sat down. "I'll have the same," he said to the waiter who'd come rushing over as soon as he'd spotted Alessandro.

"I did an article on him for our sports special on the television," Ilario told Casey. To Alessandro he said, "How are you doing?"

"Fine, thank you." He took Casey's hand and smiled at her. "How was the museum?"

"I loved it," she admitted. "I also walked around a while to see some more of the town."

"It's beautiful, isn't it?" Ilario asked. "I'm here to cover the race tomorrow. Will you be watching?"

"Yes, but from where I don't know. Everywhere I go there is a stampede for autographs or photos." He ran his hand through his short curls and sighed.

"Why don't you come to the announcer's stand we have set up for the Channel Three news?" Ilario said to him. "That way you'll be out of the crowd and in a great position to see the whole race."

"Thanks, that would be great. What do you think, Casey?"

"I think it sounds wonderful," she said, relieved they wouldn't be in the midst of the crowd.

Ilario stood up and glanced at his watch. "I'd better get moving. I'll see you tomorrow at the race. Come early and you'll dodge the worst of the crowds. Bring sandwiches and drinks—once you're there, you'll have to stay until the end. Oh, and there's one little catch."

Alessandro raised an eyebrow. "What is that?"

Ilario grinned. "Well, I saw your girlfriend first—but I concede victory to the better man. However, in compensation, I ask a little favor."

"I think I know what's coming," said Alessandro. He seemed amused. "An interview? Exclusive?"

"*Perfecto!* I knew you'd agree. *Grazie mille!* I'll see you two tomorrow. *Ciao!*"

"*Ciao,*" said Alessandro. He turned to Casey and her skin tingled. He seemed to be able to caress her with just a look from his long-lashed, amber eyes. "Where do you want to eat?"

"I don't know. Wherever you'd like," she said.

"How about here at the hotel. We can have room service. I'd rather not go out tonight. Is that all right with you?"

"Perfectly all right."

The waiter came to collect their empty glasses, hovering a bit to get a good look at his idol. Before he left, he asked Alessandro to sign his autograph on a napkin.

Alessandro complied in good humor. Then he took Casey's hand in his. "I think I'd like to go to your room for dinner. What about you?"

His fingers tightened around hers and her chest tightened in response. Since they'd arrived that afternoon, she'd been thinking about sharing a room. She knew they had two rooms and he would close the door and leave her alone if she asked him to, but she didn't want him to. He only had to glance at her and her heart started thumping. "I'd like that too," she said. She knew she was blushing. Her cheeks heated and she thought that she must be as red as the peony in the vase on the table.

Alessandro chuckled then, a warm sound that tickled her ears. "Your eyes are shining like twin stars," he whispered, his lips near hers. His fingers twined with hers and his breath was soft on her cheek.

A flashbulb went off from outside the window and the charm was broken. Casey pulled away and Alessandro swore.

"I'm sorry!" The concierge rushed over, fluttering like a nervous hen. "I'm so sorry! They must have climbed over the garden wall. I must assure you that courtyard is reserved for hotel guests. My apologies, Mr. Sottini, I am so—"

"It's all right," said Alessandro, his voice curt. He tried to smile, failed and held his hand out. "The room keys, please."

"Of course, of course!" the concierge said, bobbing his head. "Right away, sir!"

"I'm sorry," he began, when they were alone in the elevator.

"You're not going to start apologizing like the concierge, are you?" Casey asked. "It's not your fault. Don't worry about it, please." She paused. "You left the key at the front desk earlier — were you planning on going out?"

He shook his head. "No. It's customary to leave your keys with the concierge when you leave your room. There are several reasons for this." He gave a crooked smile. "One, so that when you get pickpocketed, the thief can't come back and raid your room. Two, when you're gone, the concierge can tell and take phone messages for you. And three, it's considered impolite to take your hotel key out of the hotel here in Europe." His grin widened. "Am I a good professor?"

"Yes." Casey grinned. "I liked the pickpocket reason the best. I'll definitely remember that one."

Once in Casey's room, Alessandro put his arms around her and held her tight. His heart beat beneath his shirt against her chest. "Sometimes I wish I were invisible," he said.

Casey didn't reply. Her lips sought the hollow at the base of his throat where his pulse beat strongly. She slid her hand along his jawbone, drawing his face to hers. They kissed, softly at first, lips barely touching. Sighing, she opened her mouth to his, taking his lower lip in her teeth and tugging it gently, running her tongue over the satiny softness inside. He tasted of sweet oranges with a faint tang of salt. Her knees trembled. Feelings she'd forgotten or never experienced rushed over her. Shivers ran up and down her body.

"Casey," he whispered, stepping back and staring into her eyes.

His face was flushed too, she noticed. It helped steady her nerves. She had to help him untie her halter top because his hands seemed to be shaking too much. He pushed it off her shoulders, pausing to kiss each collarbone, his lips as light as a butterfly's wings.

Her jeans followed her halter top, sliding off her hips and dropping to the floor after he fumbled with the buttons. She stood before him, wearing only her bra and underwear, feeling his gaze wander over her body. Then he unfastened her bra and tugged it away.

"*Bellissima*," he whispered.

She closed her eyes. She didn't know what she'd been expecting. All of a sudden, she had the impression of being a virgin offered for sacrifice. A smile tugged at her lips. A virgin? That wasn't quite true. But she'd only known one man.

"Open your eyes," Alessandro commanded.

She did. She was standing in front of her mirror and her body was reflected in its entirety. She was slender, but with curves. Her hips were generous and her breasts were round, with small pink nipples. She had shapely legs and as she watched, he drew his hands down her waist, over her thigh, beneath the lace of her underwear and pulled them down to her knees.

"Off," he murmured. She stepped out of them. Now, a triangle of jet-black curls made a sharp contrast to her creamy skin.

"Now it's your turn," she said, her voice shaking.

"Unbutton my shirt," he whispered. "My hands don't work anymore."

Casey was amazed to see that her hands were steady. She unbuttoned his shirt and pulled it off. His chest was broad, his shoulders wide. His collarbones stood out, as did each of his muscles. They looked as if they'd been etched in pencil into his smooth skin. She unbuckled his belt and undid his pants. Then she slid them off his hips and, crouching, pushed them down to his ankles then off.

Beneath his jeans he was bare. The curly hair on his pelvis rose in a point toward his bellybutton. His cock swelled as she looked, until it pointed straight upward. It was thick and yet long, proud as only a fully aroused cock could be. She got to her feet and ran her hands up his legs, over his hips and his sides. She closed her eyes, her hands drawing lazy circles over his hipbone and smooth dip of his groin. Holding her breath, she feathered her fingers up his cock. It quivered as she touched it.

He drew in his breath with a hiss and pulled her hard into his embrace, and she melded into his body. His erection pushed against her belly. Longing swept over her—all she wanted was to feel him plunging within her. He ran his hands down over her buttocks, stroking and massaging. Each touch took her breath away. She felt his lips move over her shoulders, her neck, and everywhere his mouth touched was like a firebrand.

"I want you," he said, his voice strained. "Say you want me too."

"I do," she gasped. It was all she could manage.

He smiled at her, his amber eyes alight. His long lashes shivered against her skin as he leaned forward to kiss her breast. As his mouth tugged on her nipple, a sharp rush of desire submerged her. She was paralyzed with delight. She hadn't known that she could be stunned into submission, but his mouth moving restlessly over her breasts and his hands stroking her sides were all that existed for her. Teasing, he slid his hand downward, rubbing it over her belly. She drew her breath in with a gasp. Then his fingers touched her soft curls.

"Tickles?" he murmured. "Shall I stop?"

"No," she whispered. "Please."

He cupped her between her legs, then he eased a finger into her damp folds. She contracted around his finger and arched her back, pressing him in deeper. He withdrew his hand and kissed her stomach.

"So lovely," he said. "Like satin." He hesitated.

"Don't stop," she breathed.

"You're trembling."

"It's been so long." Casey sighed.

"Are you sure you want to do this?" His voice was almost even.

"Yes."

"I have protection." He took a small foil packet from his wallet. "Will you put it on?" He lay back on the bed and looked at her from beneath lowered eyelashes. "I need you," he said.

As she touched him, he shivered. He closed his eyes and a moan escaped him. Casey smoothed the rubber over his stiff cock, her hands lingering, feeling him, feeling his hardness and his desire. He clutched at the bedcovers, his hips rising, thrusting toward her.

Her yearning was a sharp, empty ache between her legs. Her breathing quickened as she slid her hands up to his shoulders, pinning him to the bed. Then she spread her legs and lowered herself upon him, easing downward, until that emptiness was filled.

She closed her eyes and leaned her head on his shoulder. There was a moment of stillness, when neither wanted to move or break the spell that bound them together. Casey could sense his pulse beating in the depths of her belly. Her stomach contracted and something powerful built within her.

His arms tightened around her and he thrust his hips upward. The motion was intoxicating and she couldn't hold still any longer. The bed tilted and spun. She lost track of who or where she was. All she knew was Alessandro's body, his thrusts as he rocked her back and forth, his voice soothing her, his hands cupping her face as he drank her cries like kisses. Then he shuddered and a harsh cry escaped his throat. He bucked, digging his heels into the bed, while Casey wrapped her arms and legs around him.

They rolled over and his weight was upon her. Instinct as old as time raised her hips and they strained together. He pounded into her, each thrust accompanied by a moan. He glided in and out of her, balanced on his arms, a look of intense concentration on his face. With excruciating slowness, he withdrew until only the tip of his cock touched her, then he drove himself into her, to the very hilt. Again he slid out, teasing her, waiting until she mewed with impatience before driving into her once more. A drop of sweat slid down his temple and neck. Casey's body grew slick as she raised her hips to meet each thrust.

He chuckled and nipped her shoulder. She arched her back, driving him as far into her as she could. His chuckle turned into a groan and for a second he held still, his body shaking. "Don't move," he whispered, his voice ragged.

"Why?" She didn't need to ask. His cock twitched inside her and his face was a mask of concentration as he held himself back.

Casey closed her eyes. All her senses were pinpointed on the fullness between her legs. His cock was so big it touched her cervix and filled her wholly, but she was so aroused that her cunt pulsed in time to her heartbeat. In a minute, she was going to come. It was building, like a dam inside her about to break. Her breathing grew quicker as her nipples brushed against Alessandro's chest. Her eyes flew open as a furious throbbing began deep in her belly.

Alessandro started moving again, at first with short, shallow movements, then plunging into her, holding himself above her with his arms straight, his back arched to drive in even deeper. Now his eyes were incandescent as he gazed down on her. "*Venni,*" he said, "come with me, *venni, venni!*" He gave a wide grin and thrust again, lifting her almost off the bed.

A wave of pleasure submerged Casey. She tilted her head back and cried out. "Oh yes!" she moaned. She reached up and pulled him to her, wrapping her arms and legs around him as her body convulsed.

Alessandro's chin dug into her collarbone and he shuddered into her.

After a moment, he propped himself on his elbows, his forehead resting on hers. Their breathing slowed and evened out, and the last tremors left her body. He kissed her with butterfly touches, nibbling gently on her lips, then he lay back on the bed beside her.

Casey looked down at their legs, entwined, and she saw that his were scarred in many places. She sat up, running her hands over his ribs, his pelvis and down over his taut thighs to touch a mark near his knee. "What happened there?" she asked.

"A kick," he answered, his voice sleepy. "I have to get up. Do you mind?"

"Yes," she said and her heart swelled. "I want to feel you lying next to me forever."

"I want you with me always," he replied, kissing her again. "I'll be right back." He sat up and drew the sheet around his hips. "Beginnings can be somewhat awkward, I know that," he said, sounding apologetic. "I hope you mean it when you say you want to stay with me. I want to get to know you, I want to feel as comfortable with you as if you were a part of me. I envy those who are married for years. I want to live with a woman and see her every moment during the day and night. I want to—"

"I know what you mean," said Casey, putting her hand on his lips and hushing him. "I know how you feel. I'll stay, I promise."

His smile was blinding.

Casey lay in the bed and stared out of the windows. The moon was full and it cast a pale light into the room through the lace curtains, making arabesque shadows on the wall. Outside, laughter rose above the murmur of voices. A warm breeze crept into the room and cooled her skin. Her body was relaxed. A sleepy languor came over her and she ran her tongue over her lips—they were swollen from his kisses.

She heard water running in the bathtub and it struck her what she missed most about her life with her husband—it was all the intimate moments they'd shared without even noticing them. She realized then what Alessandro had been trying to tell her. The soft sound of someone breathing, the rattle of a toothbrush in its cup. The gentle *swish* of a shirt pulled over one's head, or the smiles shared in a mirror over a sink were all the little things a couple shares, those trivial, irreplaceable moments.

Alessandro had opened her eyes to something she'd taken for granted. It made her feel the emptiness of her life since David's death.

She rolled over and sat up, drawing her knees to her chin. She wanted someone in her life again. She smiled to herself, savoring the lingering feeling of Alessandro's lovemaking. Then the water stopped and she heard splashing as he got into the bath. Swinging her legs over the side of the bed, she stood up and stretched. A bath would be wonderful.

Casey slid into Alessandro's arms. Water sloshed over the side of the tub and spattered onto the beautiful rose-colored tiles.

"You are so beautiful," he said, cupping her chin in his hand and kissing her.

"You are so romantic," she answered. "Promise me you'll never change. Promise you'll never become one of those men who takes his wife for granted."

"Italians never take their wives for granted. We believe romance only gets better with time."

Casey laughed. "You should write brochures for the tourist industry. The country would be swarming with women seeking 'amore.'"

Alessandro raised his eyebrows. "It already is. This, my dear, is the most romantic country in the world. You'll see."

Casey gave a languorous smile. "Hmmm. I suppose I will."

"Shall we get dressed for dinner now?"

Casey looked at him from beneath lowered eyelashes. "Get dressed?" she purred. "Why on earth would I want to get dressed?" Her hand slid down his body and tickled him between his thighs. His cock swelled and hardened at her gentle touch. "I think I want to go exploring some more. We can order room service. Later."

Alessandro leaned his head back and sighed with contentment. "I think we are going to get along very well," he said.

As Casey's hand found his cock, Alessandro grew harder and caught his breath. "*Cara mia*," he moaned, arching his back. Casey giggled, a warm, tender sound, and he opened his eyes. She was grinning at him, her dark eyes alight with what looked like mischief.

"I think I have something here," she said, batting her eyelashes at him.

Alessandro closed his eyes again and shivered. Casey's touch had the most amazing effect on him. She was at the same time brazen and shy, reserved and generous. She touched him as if she'd never felt a man before, her hands hesitant, and yet, she could rouse him to a fever pitch with a simple caress. His loins tightened with desire for her. "Stop," he whispered. He opened his eyes and stared at her. "You'd better stop."

"Why?" she asked, then all of a sudden, an adorable pink flush colored her cheeks. "Oh! Protection," she said and her blush deepened.

"Luckily, I am an optimist. I have a whole box in my suitcase."

"A whole box? And how many is in a box?"

"Six."

She climbed out of the tub and, to his regret, wrapped a robe around her body, hiding its luscious curves.

"Don't leave," he said.

"Who's leaving? I'm going to poke around in your suitcase." She winked at him and came back a minute later, hiding her hands behind her back. "Which one?" she asked with a grin. Her robe was open, revealing her breasts and pointed triangle of pubic hair. She noticed his gaze and raised her eyebrows. "Are you looking at this?" Keeping her hands hidden, she lifted her foot and put it on the bidet, opening her knee to give him a glimpse of her labia.

Alessandro licked his lips. His cock was getting stiffer by the second. "The left hand," he said.

She pulled her left hand out and opened it. A foil packet glinted on her palm. "You win!" Then she opened her right hand and he laughed when she said, "I had one here too. I didn't want you to lose."

"Put it on me," he said, "please?"

Casey slid her robe off her shoulders and perched on the edge of the tub.

Alessandro lifted his hips, his erection jutting out of the water. He had to hold his breath when she pushed the rubber over his cock. Her movements were both shy and wanton. When she was done, she leaned over and slid her mouth over the tip of his cock, nibbling. He groaned aloud. The sight of her breasts and hair dipping into the water while her full lips pursed around his cock drove him wild.

She pulled back, looked at him then, not taking her eyes from his, she put one leg into the bath, then the next, straddling him. Flipping her hair out of her face, she lowered herself to her knees then grasped his cock and nestled it between her labia. She moved her hips, sloshing the bath water over the sides as she went faster. He tried to penetrate further, but she raised her hips and now her cunt was just out of his reach.

"Wait," she said. Then she started again, brushing her cunt over his cock, just hard enough so that was a constant caress. He closed his eyes, lifted his hips and gripped the side of the tub. She took her sweet time, lowering herself, taking him halfway in. Then she started moving again, in circles this time, so that he stroked her from inside. When he thought he was about to explode, he grabbed her waist and uttered a strangled cry. *"Per favor!"* he gasped and thrust into her.

She took him all the way, her slick, tight cunt sheathing itself on his cock. Now she shoved downward, not back and forth.

"Harder!" she cried, tipping her head back.

That did it. He cried out, jerking as he ejaculated into her. His hands slipped off the side of the tub with a resounding splash. Casey echoed his cry, leaning over and pressing her breasts against his chest, holding on to him. After a while she relaxed and slid off him, her face flushed, her hair damp and tangled.

"You look like a sex goddess," said Alessandro, when he could speak.

"How many rubbers did you say were in a box?" Casey asked, getting out of the tub and putting her bathrobe back on.

Alessandro was sorry to see her body disappear underneath the white robe. Her breasts were outlined against the wet cloth and her nipples showed through the cotton. He felt another sharp twinge of desire. "Pardon me? You were saying? Er, how many boxes?"

"Only one box." She smiled and shook her head. "From what I can see"—and here she leaned over and peeked into the tub—"we'll be finished with one box by tomorrow morning."

And now, it was his turn to feel his face become red.

Chapter Five

The next morning, Casey opened her eyes as pale pink light from the sunrise streamed through the windows. Next to her, Alessandro shifted and turned to face her. He smiled, reached out and touched her on the lips. "Are you awake?" he whispered.

"Yes, are you?"

"No. I'm talking in my sleep."

"Silly," she said and couldn't hide her giggle. "I didn't think you'd be up so early after last night."

"Me neither, *especially* after last night." He grinned, winced and touched his tongue to his lip. "I'm sore."

"Ha. You should talk. After last night, I don't think I'll be able to walk for a week."

He leered at her. "Oh no? So, you're not interested in another round?" He propped himself up on his elbows and looked down at her. "Maybe this time you'll win and keep me pinned. If I'm lucky," he added with a teasing grin.

"Oh yeah?" Casey raised her eyebrows. "I agree that the last bout of lovemaking was more on par with a wrestling match, but I'm not sure who won."

"You fell asleep first," he informed her gravely. "I watched you as you slept. You have the sweetest snore."

"I do not!" She hit him with a pillow.

"You do." He dodged and caught her around the waist, burying his face in her neck. "Oh, Casey, look what you do to me."

"I don't have to look...I can feel," she said with a shaky laugh. "You have a similar effect on me too, I'm afraid."

"You're afraid?" He ran his mouth down her neck and nibbled her collarbone. "Don't be afraid, I'll be gentle this time." He lifted his head and smiled. "I can be very gentle."

"I know, but I'm so sore that I'll scream if you touch me again."

"Screaming is fine, I don't mind," he said. He nuzzled her breast and sighed. "But it's too early in the morning for screams. The hotel might call the police. So we wait a while." He gave a huge yawn. "Room service?" He didn't wait for an answer but reached for the buzzer. "Two continental breakfasts in about an hour," he said. "Is that all right?" he asked Casey.

"An hour," she agreed, her hand burrowing under the covers. "But don't think you're getting away," she giggled, watching as his face grew still when she found his cock.

"Don't stop," he said with a wide grin, "until I beg for mercy."

Casey moved her fingers over his sex. At first soft, its velvety skin shivered and swelled. Alessandro's cock rose, changing shape and form until it pointed toward his belly. It was now stiff and quivering, and Alessandro tipped his head back on his pillow and let his breath out in a soft hiss as Casey pumped her hand back and forth.

With her other hand, she reached between his thighs and stroked his testicles, finding the satin-smooth patch of skin behind them. She drew little circles, marveling at its texture. His balls tightened as she tickled them and Alessandro uttered a little moan. She took his cock with both hands and encircled it, feeling little tremors shaking his body as she pumped faster.

She leaned over and kissed the tip, tasting the sharp tang of salt and clean, musky skin. She slid her lips over his cock, aware of how intimate this was. Her whole body flushed. Arousal flared in her belly and her stomach tightened with need. Alessandro stroked her hair with a hand that shook. He groaned, arching his back, and a tiny spurt of juice wet her mouth. Another pang of desire shot through her and this time there was a telltale rush of heat deep within her. She rubbed her clit against his shin, while taking his cock deeper in her throat, still working him harder and faster with her hands.

"I can't...hold back anymore," Alessandro gasped.

Casey quickened her pace, sliding her hands up and down his strong shaft, her mouth and tongue sucking and massaging his penis. She pressed her cunt harder against his shin, moving back and forth. Her clit swelled, sending tingles of excitement through her body.

When he came, he cried out. His fingers twined in her hair and he held her head while he ejaculated into her mouth. His cum hit the back of her throat while his cock twitched. A wave of pure sexual pleasure washed over her and she ground her cunt harder against his leg, a quick pulsing growing deep in her. She reached between her legs and pinched her clit, rolling it between her fingers until she came, her lips still fastened to Alessandro's cock, his hands still cupping her face while she convulsed against him.

He relaxed his tight grip and Casey pressed a kiss to the base of his cock then trailed a line of kisses to his thighs and belly. By the time she reached his chest, he had fallen asleep, a satisfied smile on his face. She leaned over and fluttered a butterfly kiss on his lips then cuddled into his arms and fell asleep.

* * * *

The knocking woke Casey up an hour later.

"Breakfast!" called a cheery voice at the door.

Casey raised her head and groaned. "What time is it?" She looked at the clock. "Seven. Coming!" she called.

She shook Alessandro's shoulder, but he just mumbled and dug his head deeper into the pillow. She smiled at him, kissed his shoulder then grabbed a bathrobe from the back of the chair and opened the door.

Breakfast was served on a linen tablecloth with crystal glasses and real silverware. Casey thanked the waiter as he left and poured herself a glass of freshly squeezed orange juice. She picked up the morning paper and settled herself on the comfortable overstuffed armchair, the table in front of her. Before she opened the paper, she took a buttery, flaky croissant and spread strawberry jam on it. Then she bit into it and sighed in delight. "This is heaven," she said and began to read.

On the front page was a picture of Alessandro and her. The picture had been taken through a window from a telephoto lens. *Their* window, to be precise. They were standing near the bed and Alessandro's arms were around Casey's waist. In the photo, his broad shoulders were visible and so was his long, muscular back tapering down to his slender waist. By chance, the bouquet of roses hid his buttocks. His body was in front of hers, but the photo clearly showed her naked shoulders and her face, glowing, as she looked at him. The headline read *Alessandro Sottini and His American Fiancée in Siena* and the article went on to say that they had 'cemented their relationship' with a stay in 'a romantic five-star hotel.'

Casey wished she could cement the photographer's camera shut. She put her half-eaten croissant back on her plate, her appetite ruined.

Casey stared at the picture again and fixed her gaze on Alessandro. He stirred but didn't wake. She put the newspaper down and wasn't surprised to see her hands were shaking. A glance at the window reassured her that the shades were drawn. Alessandro had done that when they'd turned out the lights. A pity they hadn't thought to do it sooner.

She glanced back at the picture. From a purely esthetic point of view, the photo was beautiful. If it hadn't been of Alessandro and her, she might have admired the pure lines of his body and the tempting curves, just visible, of her own body behind his.

But what would her family and friends think of this picture? Her heart started thumping and her eyes prickled with embarrassed tears. What if David's family saw this? Or one of his friends? It could cause only hurt. It was unthinkable. Perhaps she was making a monumental error.

She sat down and picked at her half-eaten croissant. The coffee pot steamed, so she made herself a cup, stirring a generous spoonful of thick cream into it. Sipping it, she cuddled deeper into the chair, feeling all of a sudden as though she were caught in a trap.

Her gaze strayed to Alessandro again. How could he bear it? Every day must be like this one, to him. She'd seen the crowd around his apartment. He had to have a bodyguard whenever he went out in public. Then Ilario's words came back to her. A soccer pro's career is short. As soon as he couldn't play and win, as soon as his formidable physique betrayed him, the crowds would vanish. And when his career ended, his fans would abandon him and he would be alone.

Casey set her coffee cup back down and slid back into bed with Alessandro. She put her arms around him and held him. He would need her when that happened. She would be there for him. Until then, well, she would just have to make sure the shutters were closed and the curtains drawn.

* * * *

Alessandro intercepted the ball, his body adjusting to the speed and weight of it without conscious thought. He could almost play with his eyes closed. He knew the size, the volume and the angles of the field. He could calculate the ball's trajectory in a split second. It was faster than thought. His instincts took over. Years and years of hard practice had honed his skills until he could shoot at the goal from anywhere and know just how to place the ball.

Right now, the opposing goalie, overconfident or perhaps too nervous, had advanced farther than he should have out into the playing area. Alessandro feinted a pass to his left then kicked the ball high, lobbing it over the goalie's head and into the goal. The man marking him, the number seven on Rome's Lazio team, gave a frustrated shout. The crowd in Torino's stadium erupted in a huge cheer. But it was a cheer tempered with disappointment. It was clear that their team was losing. The Lazio team, dressed in light blue and determined to win the championship that year, had stormed onto the field and right away scored two goals. To make matters worse, the rain didn't let up and the ground turned slick and muddy. A third goal put Lazio in the clear and Alessandro's goal came too late to do any good.

The final whistle sounded and Alessandro leaned over, hands on his knees, getting his breath back. His legs and chest ached with fatigue, but a glance around him showed that all the other players were in the same condition.

The Lazio player nearest him took off his shirt and offered to swap — Alessandro took his own off and gave it to him. The traditions of soccer were many and the uniform-trading at the end of the games was a favored one. Alessandro knew that his shirts were in demand. He also knew that the shirt was docked from his pay — but it was just a drop from the ridiculously full bucket he was offered each month to play his favorite game. He shook hands with the referees, all the while testing his knees as he cooled down.

Jogging off the field, with the Lazio shirt clutched in his hand, Alessandro was caught by three cameramen and a journalist from one of the sports stations. "You must be disappointed," were the journalist's first words to him. "What will the *squadra bianca* do now?"

Alessandro longed to push by and go take a hot shower. The weather was cool now, late September, and he was feeling the chill on his bare back. The rain didn't slacken and he debated putting on the Lazio shirt but it was drenched and icy cold. He looked at the journalist and tried to remember the man's name, but he couldn't. So he just smiled and, in a polite tone, said, "The *squadra* will have to refine her tactics a bit more. It's only the fourth game of the season."

"And it's the fourth loss," reminded the journalist.

Alessandro winced. "The third loss. We had one tied game. You must understand, although we would have liked to win, we have to be realistic. A lot of our players are new and have to get used to the team. I'm sure, as the season progresses, the *Squadra di Torino* will take her rightful place. Now, if you'll please excuse me..." He made to go by, but the journalist grabbed his arm. The cameramen, well-trained, planted themselves squarely in front of him, hemming him in.

The journalist thrust the microphone in front of him. "Alessandro, can you tell us anything about your American fiancée? Rumor has it you're planning to go to the United States to play soccer."

"That is the first I've heard of that," said Alessandro, pushing the journalist's microphone away from him. His temper was slipping, but managed to keep a bland smile on his face.

"Your fiancée —"

"I must go," said Alessandro. "Excuse me." He had to shove to get by the cameraman. He hated to do that. On film it would look as if he had been rude, but it couldn't be helped. He refused to answer personal questions. *Damn them anyway – what business is it of theirs?* He simmered with anger as he stalked down the long hallway. It was crowded with journalists, cameramen, players, coaches, guards, press agents and the various men and women who worked at the stadium, and everyone wanted a piece of him, it seemed, grabbing at his arms, peppering him with questions.

After what seemed like ages, he found his chair and sank into it and Fabricio, sitting in the next chair, tossed him a bottle of water and a dry towel. Thankful, he wiped his face off and leaned back in his chair. He didn't dare stay still too long, though. His muscles would get sore. Sighing, he stood and did some stretching exercises before heading for the showers then going to see Dimitri, the masseur.

All the players had a massage after the game. It was a short one, but it loosened up the hard-worked muscles and the masseur could tell when a knee or an ankle was weakening. He could help strained thighs and sprained ankles. While he was lying on his back, Dimitri prodding his knee, the head coach, Francisco, came into the massage room.

Zeroing in on Alessandro, he said without preamble, "I need to talk to you about something. What's this I hear about you going to America?"

Alessandro groaned. "It's not true. I heard about that for the first time tonight. I have no idea where that rumor came from."

"Oh? Don't you?" Francisco asked. He folded his arms over his chest and raised an eyebrow.

Alessandro rolled over on the table and sat up, his legs out in front of him. He winced as Dimitri touched a bruise on his shin. "That's where I was kicked today."

"Alessandro..." His coach patted his shoulder. "You know I never like to get involved with my players' personal lives...but I don't know if getting involved with this American widow is a good idea. I've never met her, but I hear she's older than you. She's from another country and the fans don't like that sort of thing."

"You always get involved with our personal lives," Alessandro said, growing more irritated. "But it has never bothered me before. Now you are stepping out of line. I realize you only want the best for the team, so consider this. I play the best when I'm happy and Casey makes me happy." He made a dismissive gesture with his hands. "Please, Francisco, forget about this. The fans will get over it. The journalists will tire of the news and I am not considering for a minute going to America to play." He grinned. "Can you see me playing soccer in Texas?"

Francisco shrugged and smiled. "Yeah, surrounded by cowboys and their longhorns. I'm glad I can always count on you to be straight with me and speak your mind, Alex." He looked around, lowered his voice and leaned close. "But believe me, the rumors flying around this stadium are very nasty, indeed. Your American fiancée is stirring up trouble...mark my words. Think about what I say, at least. There are other women out there, Alessandro, more fitting to your image."

"My *image*?" Alessandro sat up straighter and fixed his coach with a glare. "I don't give a damn about that.

I care about my game, about the team and about Casey. You know as well as I do my image will last exactly as long as my career and that could end tomorrow. Don't ask me to give up a chance to be happy with the woman I love just to save an image that is about as real as your shadow." He stopped and ran both hands through his hair, trying to get hold of his temper.

Francisco had the grace to look abashed. "I'm sorry, Alex. It's not like me to meddle." He spread his arms. "I'll tell you what, why don't you forget what I said, all right? I guess I'm still upset about losing the game."

But Alessandro couldn't forget. He replayed his coach's words over and over in his head as he drove out of the stadium. He wished Casey were with him. She had been at the game, but she'd left with Jane Leeds. He would meet them at the apartment building. The Leeds lived on the sixth floor and he was on the eighth floor.

At least something was going right. He'd get to see Casey tonight. His good humor reasserted itself and he smiled as he went into the building and pushed the button for the elevator.

* * * *

Casey sat with Jane in the Leeds' living room. She nursed a glass of scotch, but the fiery alcohol couldn't seem to warm her. A chill had settled in her bones. The paper that morning had a headline reading *Alessandro Sottini – His Fiancée Is Taking Him Away from Italy!* It went on to say that she was older than he was and the journalists treated her like some Jezebel intent on seducing their soccer star away from his own country. Where they'd gotten that idea was beyond Casey.

"Don't worry about it," said Jane, patting her knee. Her eyes were full of sympathy. "Let me tell you about what happened in England last year. One of the players married a woman twice his age and the press had a field day with it. But, you know, it blew over almost as soon as it started and they are still quite happy, I assure you."

"I appreciate you trying to make me feel better," said Casey. "But don't worry about me, really. I'll get over it and, as you say, the press will get over it."

Jane leaned back on the couch. "You don't realize, do you, just what a blow you've dealt to half the population of Italy? The female half that is. You've snared their dream man and they're devastated, believe me."

"Oh, I believe you. You should see the looks I get from the baker's daughter. Of course, most of the men think it's wonderful—I've been handing out Alessandro's autographs like candy. But I dread going to art school now."

"It's only the first week—don't worry, the fuss will die down, it always does."

Casey looked up as the doorbell sounded. "That must be Alessandro. Thank you, Jane. Will I see you next Thursday night?"

"For the game against Verona? Why, yes! Why don't you come here and we can all leave together. That way, Alessandro won't have to escort you to the players' section and the crowd won't notice you."

* * * *

"Do you remember your parents?" Alessandro asked her. He lay on his bed, an ice pack held to his knee.

Casey raised her eyebrows. "Why do you ask?"

"Just curious about you, that's all." He gave a sleepy grin. "I just want to hear the sound of your voice, I guess."

Casey smiled and lay down on her stomach next to him, propping her chin on her elbows. "They died when I was very young, so I don't remember them at all. I was raised in foster homes. But I have pictures of them."

"It must have been very difficult living with foster parents." He stroked her hair. "Were you happy?"

Casey took his hand and kissed it, holding it to her cheek. She shrugged. "It was hard… When I was little, I lived in a fantasy world where my real parents were held prisoner by a wicked witch but they would rescue me someday. I managed to get through the worst moments like that. The last foster family I lived with was my husband's family. I met him when I went to live with them. I was in junior high school and their son, David, was in college. I think I fell in love with him even before I saw him—his parents talked about him all the time and the sun rose and set on him, according to them."

"So you got married to your foster brother?" He raised his eyebrows. "Is that legal?"

Casey grinned. "Yes. It does sound strange. You have to understand, David didn't live at the house, he was away at college. The Hatters—Sam and Ellen—took me in when I was twelve and I'll always be grateful to them. They were thrilled when David and I became engaged. I don't know how many families would welcome a penniless orphan into their homes and not mind when their adored son married her. But they didn't mind and I married him with their blessings."

"Well, I should hope so!" Alessandro bristled. "I think they got the best part of the bargain."

Casey shook her head. "No, David was special. He had a gentleness about him that everyone sensed. He cared about people. He loved doing good deeds."

"How long were you married?" Alessandro asked. Casey looked at him, but his face gave nothing away.

"We weren't married that long. Four years is hardly time to get to know someone, especially as he was often away on business trips."

"What did he do?" His voice held no clue to his thoughts.

"He was a fund-raiser for about ten different charities in Ohio State. He worked with shelters for the homeless and he was always trying to fix the world, as he put it." Casey gave a little sigh and glanced at Alessandro. "You don't mind talking about him?"

He shrugged. "Do you?"

"A little." Casey sat up and took his face in her hands. "What is it?"

"I guess I'm jealous," he said. He smiled, but it faded and he gave a deep sigh. "When you talk about him, I have the impression I'm hearing about a saint and I don't know if I can compete."

Casey blinked, startled. "You? Compete with…" His bleak expression disconcerted her. "I'm sorry. It's true David was a special person, but you mustn't be jealous. If you want to know the truth…" She broke off as her cheeks grew warm. "He… His… Well, you know."

Alessandro seemed more and more interested. "His what?"

Casey gnawed on her lower lip. "His you-know-what wasn't that...talented," she blurted.

"Talented?" Alessandro's eyebrows rose. His mouth twitched.

Casey punched his arm. "Can we please change this subject?" she asked.

"All right. Case closed." Alessandro took her hand and kissed it. "Is my *you-know-what* more exciting then?"

She had no clue whether he was being facetious or not. He was looking at her with a half-smile on his lips, so she only shrugged and returned his stare. "You said case closed, and so it is," she said, lightly stroking his arm. "I don't want his memory to come between us, all right?"

"Agreed. But I can't help thinking about it." He yawned and shifted the ice pack higher on his knee. "But I promise I'll try not to be jealous anymore. Are you jealous?"

"Only of living girls who insist on throwing themselves on you and kissing you."

He appeared surprised. "Have you seen many of those around?"

"No, thank goodness." Casey laughed then sobered. "You look tired. Are you all right?"

"Don't worry," he said. "I always look this bad after a game."

Casey nodded. "It's getting late. Why don't I go back to my apartment and we'll see each other tomorrow?"

"Why don't you move in with me?"

Casey traced the velvety curves of his mouth with her fingertip. "We already talked about that. It's too soon."

"No." Alessandro's voice was stubborn. He sat up and took the ice off his knee, putting the ice pack on the floor. Then he flexed his leg, wincing as he tested it. "Help me up." He held out his hand. But when Casey took it, he pulled her onto his lap. "I want you here with me," he said, burying his face in her neck, his lips moving against her throat. "When you're away, I miss you."

"I miss you too." Casey giggled as he slipped his hand under her shirt. "That tickles."

"You're all soft and warm."

Casey shifted her weight. "I'm also heavy, don't you think?"

"You have curves," said Alessandro. "I love your shape. I can touch you, feel you, and you're comfortable when you wrap around me."

"I wrap around you?" Casey cocked an eyebrow. "Just when do I do that?"

"Hmmm. Shall I show you?" His eyes, she noticed, got darker when he was aroused. His mouth was soft. "Kiss me," he said.

Casey didn't need urging. Her lips found his and she gave a little moan as he found her bra and unfastened it. Her breasts, freed from the lace and satin, were now captive in warm hands. Casey let out a sigh as he pinched and rubbed her nipples. They rose and hardened, and she quivered with pleasure. The shiver reached into her belly and there a rush of heat between her legs. He leaned over and fastened his mouth more to hers. The swell of his cock pushed against her thighs. Passion swept over her and she arched her back, offering herself to him.

He chuckled, then, taking his hands from her breasts, he deftly undid the buttons to her shirt and pants. "You have the loveliest body," he said, a catch in his throat.

"It makes up for my face," said Casey with a shrug.

"Are you fishing for compliments?" Alessandro asked, stretched out on the bed next to her.

"I'm fishing for your fly," said Casey, with a mischievous grin.

"You found it," he said. He raised an eyebrow. "I hope the catch is to your liking."

"It's nice. Perfect," she amended, seeing his raised eyebrows. She encircled it with her fingers then slid her hand up the length of it. "It's not too thick, not too thin… It's long and strong, just how I like it."

"I was not fishing for compliments." His voice was ragged. "But I'm glad you like my cock. I've gotten quite attached to him." He broke off as she squeezed harder and pumped up and down. "That feels so nice," he said, an indrawn breath between each word.

"I've sort of grown attached to him too," said Casey, pulling his pants down.

Casey finished undressing him then stood back to admire. His body was lean and yet muscular. When she touched the tip of his erect cock, his stomach contracted and a little moan escaped his lips.

Slowly, she slid her hand over his thighs and groin, feeling each dip and swell. She closed her eyes, which heightened her sense of touch. With her fingertips, she explored the soft, smooth skin near his hipbone, then she slid her hand down toward his stomach and found a path of curly, wiry hair that led toward his sex. She kept her eyes closed. She could hear him draw his breath in with a hiss as her fingers swept lightly over his groin, tickled through his pubic hair then found his penis. She paused, resting her fingers on the base of his cock, and she felt his pulse beating at her touch. The same pulsing was echoed within her. It grew sharper, almost painful.

Her hand closed around his cock. With just a gentle butterfly touch, she ran her fingertips up and down the length of him, feeling his arousal. She marveled at how his cock could seem both hard as ivory and yet supple and satin smooth. It thickened again, getting stiffer as her fingers tightened around him. She opened her eyes, meeting his hot gaze. Little beads of sweat glistened on his forehead. He swallowed and the muscles moved in his throat.

Casey bent her head and, taking it slow, slipped her lips around the very tip of his cock. With her tongue, she tickled the rim, all the while running her hand up and down his shaft. She lowered her mouth, taking in as much as she could. He shook, trying to control his body—he clutched at the bedcovers and his breath came in quick gasps. Casey loved the saltiness of him, the warmth of his skin, the smooth, satiny feeling of his body. She could sense him losing control. Already, small tremors shook him and a small spurt of salty-sweet juice tickled her tongue. He took her shoulders and pushed her away.

"Wait," he said. His eyes were feverish.

Casey's eyelids were heavy. Her whole body was soft and warm as honey seemed to flow through her veins instead of blood. Alessandro pressed her down onto the bed and leaned over her. His mouth found her nipples and she gave a cry. "Hush," he whispered, trailing his hand over her waist, down her hips, then dipping between her legs. Instinctively, she raised her pelvis and he opened her, slipping his index finger into her cunt, rubbing his thumb on her clitoris. She was so wet his fingers slipped over her outer and inner lips. They were swollen with need, as if they wanted to swallow him whole.

"Oh!" she cried, bucking against him. She wanted him to slide the whole weight of his body against her, to have his fingers and cock take her. She needed to feel something penetrate her. Her cunt throbbed, like a hungry mouth opening and closing, begging to be stuffed full. She grinned at the analogy then moaned in frustration as he withdrew his finger.

"No, slow down, not yet," he said, his mouth against her breast. He tugged at her nipple with his lips, sending delicious electric shocks through her. He put one finger, then two within her, moving them slowly but hardly penetrating at all. Then he brushed the palm of his hand over her outer lips, teasing.

"Please," she gasped. "I want you now!"

"I need to put a rubber on," he said, his voice ragged.

"Hurry!" she almost screamed.

He complied, sliding over her and nudging her legs apart with his knee. Then he lowered himself into her, sheathing himself in one smooth thrust. His breath was coming in gasps as he tried to control himself.

Casey couldn't wait. There was a pressure growing in her body, threatening to explode. She grabbed his hips and pulled him into her. "Harder," she gasped.

They strained against each other, their bodies slick and sliding as they rocked back and forth. A cry tore from Casey's throat as her orgasm shook her. Waves of pleasure submerged her. Alessandro gave a harsh cry and bucked into her, his whole body quivering with his release.

Afterward, they lay still and let the silence wash over them. Just before Casey fell asleep, Alessandro pressed her hand to his lips. "Sweet dreams," he whispered.

Chapter Six

The telephone woke her. It rang and rang until Alessandro answered, his voice blurred with sleep. He spoke for a moment then replaced the phone. "Good morning," he said in a soft voice, smiling at Casey.

Casey sat up, the sheets falling in disarray around her. She ran her fingers through her hair. "Who was that?"

"My wake-up call. I have to go to the stadium for a practice this morning." He sat up straighter and stretched, showing off his wonderfully lean torso and smooth muscles.

"Keep that up and I'm going to be late for class," she said, giving him an appreciative glance.

He grinned. "I'll have Tonio drive you. What do you want for breakfast?"

"What do you have?" Casey gave a rueful grin. "I haven't had time to visit your kitchen yet."

"What? I didn't give you the grand tour of my palace?" Alessandro feigned surprise.

"No, you've been most remiss as a host."

He scratched his head. "I suppose if I'd been able to drag you out of the bedroom, I would have been able to show you a bit more. But you cuddled right up in my bed and I didn't have the heart to move you."

Casey giggled. "I wasn't planning on staying—it was a trap."

He smirked at her then leaned over and kissed her. "Yes, a trap. And you fell right into it—with cries of delight, if I'm not mistaken."

She laughed, kissing him back. Her nipples tightened in response. "You Italians are so seductive. How could I resist?"

His face lit up. "Seductive. I like that." He posed, his hand on his chest. "It goes with our education. When we're born, our mothers tell us we're the most amazing little boys they've ever seen. Then, as we're growing up, our mothers never tell us we're ugly or worthless. No, they make sure we know that the sun only rises so it can see us and at night, it sends the moon and stars to watch over us. Little Italian boys are the most spoiled creatures on earth."

"And what about little Italian girls?" Casey matched his bantering tone, her eyes sparkling.

"Their fathers dote upon them. They buy them presents, sweets and ribbons, everything a little girl loves best. They know they are their fathers' little princesses and a little Italian girl is always happy because she knows she's the most beautiful little girl in the world. Italian children, in general, are very spoiled. We adore our children, but we make sure they are always well-dressed and well-behaved." He nodded and put his arm over her shoulders.

"I have noticed that the children here are particularly well-mannered," said Casey, amused by his lecturing.

"So, when will we start our own family?" Alessandro murmured, leaning over and kissing her bare shoulder. He trailed his lips over her collarbone and down to one breast. He took the nipple in his mouth and sucked on it.

Delighted shivers coursed through her body. "We'll talk about that later," she gasped, as he reached beneath the covers and found her cleft. She opened to his touch, lying back on the pillows. He gave her a boyish grin and moved his restless mouth to her other breast. Her nipples hardened and ached, and she gave a little cry as he nibbled then seized one with his teeth and tugged on it.

He stroked her, his fingers dancing over her soft pubic hair, parted her labia and gently eased into her slick passage. Sparks of desire stung her as he found her G-spot. Then he rubbed it, moving his finger side to side, while he reached down with his other hand and found the small nub that was her clitoris. It was so sensitive from their lovemaking the night before that she couldn't suppress a gasp.

"Sore?" he asked, concern in his voice. He withdrew his hand.

"No! It's all right, just be gentle," she begged. She took his hand and pressed it between her legs, arching her back so that he could enter her more easily. He pushed first one finger into her, then two. The sensation was exquisite. Casey grabbed his wrist and held it, accompanying his movements.

"I want to feel you coming with my hand," he said. He picked up the pace, thrusting his fingers in and out of her cunt, brushing his thumb like a feather against her stiff clitoris. Her flesh swelled, getting more sensitive as a wave crested over her.

She was so wet that his fingers were slick and slippery. She arched her back, pressing herself harder against his hand, her passion growing stronger and stronger until she couldn't control it any longer. Her body seemed to explode as her world was reduced to the sensations Alessandro was giving her. Little darts of electricity flowed from his hands into her body, or maybe it was the other way around. She couldn't tell. Her head was spinning, her breath coming in little gasps. Then her belly was convulsing and there was a mad pulsing within her. As the feeling reached a climax, she tipped her chin back and grabbed at his hands, holding them still, pushing them hard against her as she ground her pelvis against him. She could feel her muscles contracting around his fingers, the throbbing growing, a rush of hot liquid as she came, then subsiding to a few little tremors.

"Oh Lord," she whispered when she got her breath back.

Alessandro leaned over her, a grin on his handsome face. "You called me?" he said.

"Yes, I did," Casey answered, giving him a contented smile. "Now, I will definitely be late for school."

"No, Tonio will get you there on time. Why don't you go shower while I get breakfast ready? I'll call Tonio and have him here in half an hour, all right?"

"You are an angel," said Casey, looping her arms around his neck and kissing his lips.

His face softened as he looked at her. "Casey, I was serious when I spoke of starting a family. I want you to stay with me. I love you, I think I've loved you from the moment you mispronounced my name and dropped your folder on my foot. I want you to think about it, please? I know, I know…" He held up his hand. "Don't say it. You're American, you're older than I am and you don't want to make a commitment so quickly. You've been saying that all month."

Casey gathered the sheets around her. She wanted to say yes, she longed to stay with Alessandro forever, but her mind was shouting at her to be cautious, not to get hurt again. She cupped his face in her hands. "Please, let me get used to the idea, all right?" she asked.

His disappointment showed through his smile, but he just nodded and said, "All right. Take your time." He kissed her on the lips then trotted into the kitchen. Soon the tempting aromas of fresh oranges, toast and coffee filled the air.

* * * *

Tonio dropped her off at the school and she waved as she hurried into the building. She felt as if her position were tenuous, even though she had every right to be there. Sure, she'd earned the award, and sure, she had an all-expenses-paid tuition. Casey remembered thinking she'd won the lottery the day the certified letter had come in the mail, telling her congratulations, she'd been awarded a year's scholarship. But now, as she slipped into her place behind her easel, she thanked the heavens Tonio drove fast and she'd arrived on time. For the first time, she had the impression she was much older than and far different from the other students. She tried to be as inconspicuous as possible.

"Bitch," said a girl as she walked behind Casey.

Casey whirled around in shock. "I beg your pardon?" she said, not sure she'd heard right. To be sure, the students had been less than friendly, but no one had been hostile before today.

"Why don't you just go home? There is nothing for you here," said the girl between clenched teeth.

Casey was caught off guard by the girl's venomous expression. "I'm studying art here, like you," she said, a frown on her face.

"You should do it back in America and leave Alessandro alone! You hear?" hissed the girl, who turned and stalked off to her place.

Casey bit the inside of her cheek to keep from showing her distress. She clipped her paper over her easel and smoothed it, trying to find some of the joy and enthusiasm from the first time she'd walked into this classroom. The class was fascinating, but she couldn't concentrate. The other students' animosity hung like a shadow upon her.

* * * *

As she got out of the cab, a flashbulb went off right in her face. She staggered backward and was nearly hit by a young man on a scooter. By chance, he only grazed her. As it was, she was thrown to the ground.

Apologizing profusely, the photographer had the decency to help her to her feet, while the taxi driver shook his fist at the motorbike and shouted—a thing the Italians loved to do.

"*Mille pardons, signora*," said the photographer, then he dashed off as well.

"What the...?" Casey stared after him, perplexed, until the taxi reminded her of his fare. "Oh, sorry. Here you are." She dug into her purse for some lire then walked up the stairs to her apartment, her head spinning.

She didn't find out why her head hurt until she looked in the mirror. A huge bruise marred her forehead. She'd hit it when she'd fallen and hadn't noticed. Well, her arm hurt more and there was a bruise on her leg, too. With a sigh, she undressed and took a long shower, waiting until the hot water gave out before grabbing her towel and wrapping up. Then she made some soup.

The day had worn her out and she was thankful to fall into her bed, but not before checking her messages. There were three. One was from Alessandro. She replayed the tape five times, just for the warm sound of his voice. "Hi, Cassandra," he began. He loved to tease her with her full name. "I miss you already and you've only been gone a few hours. I miss you and my bed looks positively desolate." He paused and Casey closed her eyes to picture him as he spoke — seeing his handsome face and his hands that were never still. "I'm leaving tomorrow morning for training camp. I'll be back in three days. I'll call you when I come back. *Ciao, bella.*" He was silent a moment, then he said, softly, "*Ti amo.*"

Casey sighed. Three days seemed an eternity to her now.

The second message was from Ilario. It had been a while since she'd heard from him. He wanted to thank her for helping him get the interview with Alessandro and told her that his article was coming out soon — he'd let her know when. He also said she should call him, as he had a few questions to ask her.

She looked at her watch — it was almost eleven p.m., so she decided to call him the next day. The last message was from her father-in-law. Her heart sped up when she heard his voice. He'd been the one to break the news of David's death to her and now each time he called, for some silly reason, it unnerved her.

"Casey, this is Sam. I was just calling to say that Ellen and I are getting ready to visit and I wanted to give you the dates. Call me, or email me. Hope you're doing well. See you soon, honey."

Casey stared at the machine. Tears pricked her eyes. Sam and Ellen were more than in-laws. They had been her foster parents and they loved her dearly. She sniffed and rubbed her face. *Fatigue is making me maudlin*, she decided. Tomorrow she'd get everything sorted out.

* * * *

The telephone woke her from a deep slumber. Her hand groped for the receiver. "Hello?" she said, clearing her throat and rubbing her eyes.

"I'd like to kill you," said a soft voice, then the line went dead.

Casey groaned and hung up. She rolled over and dropped off to sleep again, too exhausted to realize what had happened. A while later the phone rang again. Again the soft voice whispered, "I'd like to kill you." Then the line went dead.

Casey sat up, all traces of sleep gone. The clock on her table said three a.m.

She swung her legs over the side of the bed and put on her bathrobe. Her hands shook so that she could hardly tie the belt. The voice had sounded feminine, she thought, and malevolent. She sat undecided for only a second, lifted the receiver and dialed the police. Half her mind felt ridiculous. The other half was terrified.

"Hello, this is Casey Hatter. I'm calling because I've been getting threatening phone calls tonight, and I... Yes, that's right, Cassandra Hatter. Yes, that's me." She frowned. The police officer had wanted to know if she was the American woman he'd read about in the papers. When she said yes, he told her to change her phone number as soon as possible.

"Yes, I'll do that, thank you −" A crash interrupted her words and she uttered a shrill scream. To the detective's frantic questions, she could only answer, "I don't know! Someone just threw a rock through my window!" She couldn't hold back her tears.

She waited at the door until the police car arrived, its blue lights flashing off the windows in the buildings on her street.

"I'm so sorry about all this," she said, letting the inspector into her apartment.

He looked at her in amazement. "You're sorry?"

Casey nodded and stuck out her hand. "For all the trouble. Yes. I'm Casey Hatter." She clutched her robe around her waist, too unnerved to care about her appearance.

"Detective Zucchini." He shook her hand. "Now, Miss Hatter, tell me what happened."

"That rock came crashing through my window, that's all."

"Did you hear a car or a motorbike?"

"No." Casey shook her head. "I didn't. I was on the phone and it scared me too much, sorry."

"That's all right. Let me see the rock."

Casey pointed and the detective went to the sparkling debris of her window and picked up a large rock. "There's something attached to it," he said. "It looks like a message."

"I didn't look. What does it say?" asked Casey, her voice strained.

The detective unfolded a piece of paper taped to the rock and read, "American whore. You better go back to your own country. Leave our soccer players alone. He's too good for you." The detective grimaced. "Do you have any idea who could have done this?"

For the first time that night Casey managed a wry grin. "Just any one of the unmarried females crazy about Alessandro. That makes about a million...so you have your work cut out for you." Her smile wobbled.

"We'll keep this and check for fingerprints." He pointed to her head. "Did you get that bruise when the rock came through your window?"

"No." She touched her forehead. "I got knocked down by a motorbike. I'm sorry about all this," she added.

The detective looked up at her, surprise on his face. "You keep saying that. You mustn't apologize. It's not your fault our biggest soccer star fell in love with you. However, I would consider moving into another apartment now. You should be in a guarded residence." He spoke with authority.

"I could never afford that," said Casey. She noticed his concerned look and said, "Don't worry, I'll talk to Alessandro, maybe he'll have an idea that would help."

That seemed to reassure him and he bade her good night. "Leave the telephone off the hook," he said. "If you need anything else, don't hesitate to call. I'm going to ask a patrol car to stay on your street tonight, so don't worry about anything." He held up his hand before Casey could speak. "Do not say you're sorry one more time! It's not your fault and I'm more embarrassed by this than you are, believe me. I have a hard time believing soccer fans would stoop so low."

Casey smiled. "Thank you, Detective Zucchini."

When he left, she went back to bed but she couldn't sleep. She made herself a cup of coffee and watched as the dawn turned the sky pink. The sun rose over the Piedmont Mountains and the city was gilded in pale light. Casey finished her coffee then went to take her shower and brace herself for another day.

* * * *

Alessandro tried to call Casey, but her number didn't work. A recording told him it wasn't in service anymore. That didn't worry him—the phones were often out of order. But he didn't have the number at the training camp to give her and that put him in a bad mood. He got back to his apartment just as the phone was ringing, but it wasn't Casey.

His phone rang all the time, even when he was in the shower. *Especially* when he was in the shower, he thought. He waited for the answering machine to pick up the call, but the phone kept ringing. Perhaps it was Casey! He dashed out, but when he went to answer, it had stopped ringing. Puddles of water showed where he'd dashed out of the shower. He dropped the towel he'd held around his waist onto the floor, wiping up the mess. Then he ran his hand through his hair and found it still full of shampoo. He peered closer at the offending answering machine and sighed. The recorder was full—that was the problem. He counted the messages under his breath. Thirty. The maximum.

He glared at the phone and pressed the message button. The last two caught his attention. "Alessandro, we're waiting for this week's answers to the letters your fans have sent you. Could you email them to us as soon as possible? Thank you." *Click! Beep!* "Alessandro, darling! It's me, Gloria. You haven't called in ages. I don't believe a word of what is written in the papers. I know you too well. Darling, call me the second you get this message. *Ciao.*"

There were good and bad points to recording machines, Alessandro reflected. Bad, because they let people like Gloria call and leave messages. Good, because at least he didn't have to talk to her himself. He resolved to email the magazine that evening. But what was he going to do about Gloria? He chewed his lip and brooded. She had been his date for most of the society outings his press agent had organized. She was perfect for the role—a starlet just launching her career as a film actress—and she had the added attraction of being gone often. She'd made it clear from the beginning that she was in it for the publicity and her career came *'numero uno.'*

True, she'd become a bit clingy a few months ago. She'd made a scene in that restaurant, but then she'd apologized and said it was just nerves. When had he seen her last? Five months ago, more or less. So what did she want now? Still gnawing his lower lip, he dialed her number.

In a resigned voice, he said, "Gloria. It's Alessandro. What do you want?"

"Alessandro!" she cried. "I have such great news!"

"What news?" he asked.

"Remember that calendar you and your club made a few years ago? Well, I bought the rights to it and we're going to reissue it. Isn't that fabulous?"

The breath left his chest in a whoosh. "What did you say? No, forget that. Why, Gloria?"

Her voice was malicious. "You thought you could just dump me and forget all about Gloria. Well, lover boy, you won't be able to forget anymore. *Ciao.* Have fun with your homely little housewife."

Alessandro dropped the phone onto the floor. It hit with a crash and little pieces flew everywhere. *The problem with Italian tiles,* he thought dispassionately, *is that they are as hard as Gloria's heart.* Damn her anyway. He rubbed his hair and noted the shampoo still in it. How was he going to break this particular bit of news to Casey? He sighed and headed back to the shower, emotions churning his stomach. He was pissed at Gloria, worried about Casey, and all of a sudden he was afraid that he could lose her.

* * * *

It was late, almost midnight. Casey had gone to another soccer game and this one had been worse than the ones before. As soon as she had been spotted, whistles and catcalls sounded. Then some people had stretched out a banner, on which was written in lurid red, *Casey Go Home!* Other banners unfurled around the stadium as if on cue and they all told her in no uncertain terms to leave the country.

Jane had been sympathetic and supportive, even when a soda can had flown into their section of the stands. It came close to hitting Jane on the arm, but she'd stayed next to Casey, even though Casey had begged her to sit elsewhere. During halftime she'd said she wanted to go home, but Jane and Dario's young Argentine wife, Maria-Sophia, wouldn't let her.

"Come on, Casey, you have to be strong," Jane had told her, her face determined.

Maria-Sophia spoke up with a firm tone. "*Sí*, Jane is right, you have to be a strong woman. In Argentina, the fans can be very difficult too. It's the Latin blood. Sometimes too hot!" She took Casey's hand. "We soccer wives have to stick together. Okay?"

Casey nodded. She was grateful, but she still felt awful.

"I'm so sorry about this, Jane. I can't believe someone threw something at me and almost hit you," Casey had apologized, as another round of angry whistles started.

It hadn't helped that the team lost, again, and that Alessandro limped off the field at the end of the match.

She had been glad to go back and wait for him at his apartment, but she was so wrung out that she was dropping off to sleep on the sofa when he came in at last.

She woke up when he touched her lightly on the cheek. "How's your leg?" she asked, rubbing her eyes and blinking. Just the sight of him raised her spirits. He sat next to her and put his arm around her shoulders. She leaned into him, nuzzling his neck.

"All right, although a little sore." He frowned and took a deep breath. "I have to tell you something," he said to Casey.

"What is it?" She saw his expression and her heart gave a frightened skip. "Come on, it can't be that bad," she said, sitting up straighter. "It's not about another woman or something is it?"

"Well, no. No, it's not about another woman. For me, there is only you."

"You're not married, in love with someone else or being blackmailed by the mother of your love child, are you?" She smiled, trying to coax a smile from him, but he still looked grim.

"No, there is no secret marriage, child or lover," he said.

"Well, that's all right then," she said. "What can be so bad?"

He cleared his throat. "Actually, I posed for a calendar."

"That's nice." Casey wrinkled her nose. "What's so bad about that?"

"I was naked," he said, a blush starting to creep up from his neck.

"You were what?" Casey asked. At least she tried to ask. Her voice came out a squeak.

Alessandro ran his hand through his hair. His face was a bright shade of pink now. "It was a long time ago and I was in a different club. It was to raise money, well — it was for a good cause," he said.

"What cause?" Casey didn't want to laugh. She was afraid to hurt his feelings. But she was relieved it was nothing but a sexy calendar.

"The money all went to the club… It was a public club with lots of programs for kids."

Casey closed her eyes and a smile tugged at the corners of her mouth. "I forgive you, on one condition."

"Anything," said Alessandro.

"I want one."

There was a pause, then he said, "You want one?"

"Of course. You won't mind if I put it in my bedroom, will you?" she teased. "Can I order one?"

"Um, you'll be able to get one soon, I think."

"Soon?" She raised her eyebrows. "Alessandro, I thought you said you posed for this a while ago."

"I did, it was a long…" Looking at her, he continued, "It all began with Gloria."

"Who?" Casey was caught off guard. Alessandro got off the couch and started pacing. He looked upset and she started to get a bad feeling about the whole story, especially about Gloria.

"Gloria Donatelli. She's an actress. She was my date a few times, but there was nothing between us," he added in a hurry. "At least, I didn't think there was anything between us but maybe she did, because she got all upset about me dating you. To make a long story short, she bought the rights to the photos and she's going to reissue the calendar."

Alessandro stood in front of her, a troubled frown on his face. After a few moments, she started to chuckle. "I don't mind," she said. "I never thought I'd make a starlet jealous."

"Good." The relief in his voice surprised her.

She raised her eyebrows. "It's not important," she said. "What's a little pin-up calendar? I mean, you put up with the booing and the catcalls when I come to your soccer games, so why should I mind about a couple pictures? You told me you didn't care about Gloria. *I* have you, she doesn't."

He sat down next to her and drew her into her arms. "Oh, Casey, I'm so sorry about all this. I don't mind the banners and catcalls for me — I hate them for your sake. It kills me to think that your feelings are hurt and I hope with all my heart the people doing that stop. If there was anything I could do — give a conference — an interview… Maybe I'll call Ilario and ask for a televised interview, what do you think?"

She shook her head. He was offering to expose his private life to the media — something he detested. Tears pricked her eyes. "You don't have to do that. Besides, I think it would be like throwing fat on the fire."

"You think it would make it worse?"

"Yes." She pulled him closer and kissed his temple, letting her lips linger on the strong pulse that beat there.

"What can I do to make it better?"

Casey gave a sultry smile. "That is the easy part," she said.

"So tell me, I'm listening," he said, his mouth quirked.

"Not here. Follow me." She stood and led him into the bedroom. "This is where you make me feel better," she whispered, her voice soft.

"All right, but lie down and don't move," he said, his voice as hoarse as hers was soft.

She swallowed, her mouth suddenly dry. Alessandro had the most extraordinary effect on her. Whenever he touched her, little pangs of desire stabbed her and she could feel herself getting wet and aroused.

She drew a deep breath and shivered as he ran his hands over her blouse then unbuttoned it, easing it off her shoulders. He stopped and kissed her collarbones, then he tossed her blouse onto a chair. Grinning, he reached behind her and undid her bra. He drew it off, pausing to rub the red marks beneath her breasts and arms where the elastic had pressed into her skin. Her nipples were aching for his touch, but he teased her, stroking the insides of her arms and beneath them, tickling her. He stroked the soft skin in the hollow of her underarm where it was so sensitive that the slightest touch sent shivers along her back. She sighed and shifted, trying to angle her breasts into his hands.

"No, don't move," he said and trailed his fingertips across her collarbone and along her jaw.

He shifted position, getting more comfortable, then he resumed caressing her under her arm, running his fingers down the length of her arm to her hands, then back up again. Her nipples were hard now and her breasts heavy, waiting for his touch.

He slid her jeans and underwear off. When she clenched her legs, she could feel her labia rub together, hot, slick and wet. "Don't move," he reminded her, kissing the insides of her thighs. Then, taking his sweet time, he nibbled her skin up to her hips, over her stomach and finally to her breasts. He raised his head and smiled at her. "Do you want me to touch them?" he asked, a teasing note in his voice.

"Yes!" cried Casey. She wanted to move, wanted to throw her arms around him and rub her body along his, but, mindful of his words, she lay still.

Alessandro lifted each breast and gently rubbed her nipples with his thumb. He bent over and suckled her, drawing her breast as far into his mouth as he could, tickling her with his tongue. Her skin burned beneath his caress. His mouth was hot as it traveled over her skin. His tongue was agile, prodding and searching as he licked her. Warmth seemed to flow from his fingers as he reached downward. He fondled her hips and reached behind to her buttocks, his hands moving up and down, while he tugged harder and harder on her nipples with his lips. She writhed, rubbing herself harder against his legs, parting her thighs, trying to bring him into contact with her throbbing cunt. It ached with desire.

"Whoa, slow down," he said. "I'm in no hurry, are you? Besides, you're not supposed to be moving, remember?"

Her breath was coming in short gasps by the time he sat up and knelt between her legs. He tugged his own shirt off, baring his sleek midriff and smooth muscles.

The sight of him made Casey want to climb into his skin. He shrugged out of his jeans. *Oh Lord.* She wanted to move right then. How she wanted to move! She wanted to levitate right off the bed and impale herself on his beautiful, erect cock.

He grinned at her expression. "I can read your mind," he teased.

"I certainly hope so," Casey said.

Still kneeling between her legs, he slid his hands up over her thighs to her hips and stroked her from her shoulders to her knees. She caught her breath with a hiss as he tickled the gentle dip where her hip met her stomach. Then he tickled her mons, twining his fingers gently in her pubic hair. Another pang of pleasure made her stomach muscles clench. She closed her eyes as his hot breath touched her inner thigh. He kissed the inside of her knee, nipping it and swirling his tongue over the soft skin. He parted her legs.

She lay there, offering herself to him, and imagined her labia opening like a rose. Deep in her cunt, twinges of desire throbbed in time to her heartbeat. And when he lowered his lips to the soft mound of curls between her legs and licked hard, she gave a little mew of delight. His fingers parted her flesh and his tongue dove into her cleft, licking her outer and inner labia, probing into her passage, deeper, as he pressed his mouth to her cunt.

"Oh!" she cried as he slid his hands under her buttocks and pulled her closer to him. He nibbled at her sensitive nub, then, groaning her name with pleasure, he probed again into her. He massaged her clit with his tongue, sucking at it, driving her wild with erotic feelings she'd never before experienced. She'd never felt wanton before, but now she knew what wanting really meant. Her legs, her body and her cunt all open wide for him to lick, suck and take with his fingers, mouth and cock. He swept his tongue back and forth between her labia and her clit, as she became slick and swollen with desire. Her arms and legs were heavy and her breath was coming in great gasps. Pressure built deep within her — it descended lower and a sudden rush of heat gushed from her cunt, the throbbing exploding into a starburst. A cry tore out of her throat and she ground herself into him, begging for more.

He ran his hands over her thighs then plunged his fingers into her, spurring her contractions on by rubbing her G-spot. He leaned over her, his eyes bright with excitement.

"Please!" she begged him. "Take me!"

He laughed softly. "Are you sure?" He wiggled his fingers inside her.

Her cunt stretched tight, full. How many were there? She couldn't tell — two, three? Four? "Oh!" she cried, as he withdrew his hand and attacked her with his mouth again. His lips were so hot, his tongue so agile — she crested and came again, her body shaking with her orgasm. Panting, she lay on her back and gazed at her lover. He leaned down and kissed her, his lips sweet and musky with her scent and taste.

Then he reached over to his bedside table and got a rubber. He put it on, his hands slippery with her juices. "Now you can move," he said, his voice husky.

He rose and, in a smooth movement, sheathed himself all the way into her body. Joined with her, he held still, letting her contractions stroke his stiff cock. Buried deep within her, his cock got bigger, thicker, then Alessandro uttered a strangled moan and thrust into her, harder and harder, bucking against her.

They rolled over and he lay on his back, lifting his hips high. Casey grasped him between her thighs and rode him like a horse, sliding back and forth. She balanced on her knees, leaning over and holding him by the shoulders. The leverage was terrific and he hit her womb with every long, hard stroke. He clutched at her breasts, kneading them, then he arched his back, crying out with his release.

He began to spurt inside her. His spasms pushed her over the edge again and she joined him, writhing against him as her own orgasm spun her away. His stomach convulsed beneath her own and deep in her cunt, his cock jerked and twitched. She uttered a surprised cry as another wave of throbbing shook her. It seemed that each time one of them moved, each time skin touched skin, a new bout of pleasure submerged them.

After what seemed like ages, the tremors faded. Taking deep breaths, Casey leaned against Alessandro. Her body shuddered with spent desire.

Alessandro's body was slick with sweat. A drop ran down his neck and glistened in the hollow of his throat. His chest, his belly, his thighs and even his hair were damp. With a groan, he took off the rubber, letting it fall to the floor. Casey reached over and lifted a curl off his forehead. "You're hot," she said.

"Thanks," he said. Then laughed. "No. I know what you mean. It is hot. Shall I turn on the fan?"

She chuckled. "No, let's go take a shower together instead."

"Casey?"

"Hmmm?"

"Are you trying to kill me? You are mad about the calendar, aren't you? And you've decided to kill me with sex."

Casey sat up and stared at him lying on the bed, arms and legs akimbo. He looked like a fallen angel. A very sexy fallen angel.

Her breasts started to tingle again. Smiling, she reached down and tweaked his penis. "I bet *he* won't be complaining," she said.

He glanced at her hand and gave a snort. "That little guy is a traitor. Don't parley with him. I'm the boss."

"Oh?" Casey tightened her fingers around his cock and she gave a couple of firm squeezes. To her delight, he responded by swelling in her hand. "I see what you mean," she said.

Alessandro closed his eyes. "I thought you said shower?"

Casey giggled. "How about shower later?" She couldn't wait another minute. Already the telltale throbbing grew in her cunt.

"I'm going to run out of rubbers so I'll have to go buy more," said Alessandro, joking. "You're going to ruin my health *and* my bank account."

"You know, I only ever slept with my husband and I'm on the pill," she said, looking at him from beneath her lashes. She wasn't sure if this was the right time to bring this up, but she wanted to.

"What are you trying to say?" Alessandro propped himself on his elbows and cocked an eyebrow at her. "Oh. About the rubbers." He gave a crooked grin. "Well, I can assure you that with all the medical exams and blood tests we have to take for soccer, I am completely free of any diseases." His face became more serious. "Do you want to forgo the rubbers from now on? Is that what you're trying to say? Are you okay with that?"

For an answer, Casey turned her back to him and straddled his legs. She looked back at him from over her shoulder, rose then impaled herself onto his erect cock. Now there was nothing between them. His skin was like hot satin stroking her from the inside. Sensations were heightened and she clenched her muscles around him, his cock filling her and stretching her.

She heard his gasp as she sheathed herself to the hilt, then, balancing on her heels, she moved up and down, up and down. Her back to him, she leaned forward, letting his cock stroke her inside from another angle. By moving her hips, she discovered she could vary the angle of penetration and feel new sensations in different parts of her body.

She hooked her chin on her shoulder and looked back at Alessandro. He was feasting his eyes on the sight her buttocks made as she leaned over and opened her legs wide. She turned forward and lifted herself off him, then slid back down again. She grabbed his ankles for control and thrust herself onto his cock. From this position, she moved faster, plunging up and down until contractions started in her womb, signs of her immediate orgasm.

She paused, trying to control herself, but she was already teetering at the brink, and when Alessandro arched his back, thrusting into her to the hilt, she began to shatter. She lay back, full-length on him, while he reached down, stroking and rubbing her clitoris with his thumb until she exploded with a rush of liquid heat. Alessandro shuddered, spending himself, clutching at her as he ejaculated into her. With something like a sob, he held her while his body rocked.

Chapter Seven

Casey puttered around her apartment. It was early and she was waiting for the coffee to finish perking as she peeled and ate a sweet sanguine orange. She had finished the orange and was just about to go to the bakery when the phone rang.

"Hello?"

"Casey! It's Ellen. How are you?"

Casey grinned. "I'm fine, Ellen, thank you. How are you and Sam doing?"

"We're fine—and you'll never guess where we are!"

"Where?"

"In Rome!"

"But, when you emailed, you said you were coming at Christmastime."

"We decided it would be better to come while it was still nice weather. We just arrived yesterday. We're in Rome for three days, then Florence, and we'll be in Turin next Wednesday. I'm looking forward to you showing us around the city!"

Casey blinked. "You're in Italy?"

"Yes, isn't it wonderful? Sam and I have been talking about it for ages and now we're finally here. We're at the Hassler Hotel in Rome and the view is incredible. I can see right across the river to the Vatican!"

"That's great!" Casey laughed. It was a surprise, but she had missed them. It was wonderful they were here. She drew a deep breath. "Where will you be staying in Turin?"

"Oh, Casey, I hope you'll be able to find a nice place for us. Sam and I want a five-star hotel, with a view of the mountains."

"That won't be a problem. Let me know what time your plane arrives and I'll pick you up."

"We'll be there—hold on..." Casey heard the sound of a keyboard clicking. "Okay, I found the email reservation. We arrive on Wednesday morning, eight thirty, Air Italia flight 080. I'll send you the info when we hang up."

"That will be perfect. How long are you staying?" Casey smiled. Ellen sounded so excited.

"A week, then we fly back to Ohio." Ellen paused. "I hope we're not creating any problems for you by dropping in like this. I know we were supposed to come for Christmas, but we wanted to enjoy seeing Italy in the sunshine."

She sounded worried and Casey hastened to reassure her. "Oh no! Of course not. I'm looking forward to seeing you on Wednesday."

"Bye, honey."

"Goodbye, Ellen." Casey hung up the phone and looked at her kitchen wall. Hanging on it, in all his glory, was Alessandro. Casey had seen the calendar in the magazine shop. She'd only wanted to buy the one, but the thought of anyone else having the calendar suddenly struck her as terrible, so she'd bought them all. She would have run around the city and bought every last one, but this was all her budget could afford. She gazed at the image of Alessandro standing with nothing but a soccer ball hiding his cock and frowned. What were Sam and Ellen going to think of Alessandro? What would Alessandro think of them?

She sighed and picked up her portfolio. It was time for school. She would get through this day, then she'd decide what to do with the Hatters. At least there were no more calendars in the shop at the corner.

* * * *

If only everything could be so easy. In school, all the girls had the calendar hanging from their easels. Most of them made faces at her, or sneered as she walked by. No one had made any attempt to be friendly. Even the boys had stopped asking her for Alessandro's autograph and the mutters she heard were more along the lines of the newspaper headlines — all of which had taken to blaming her for the Squadra di Torino's spectacular losing streak. Since getting trounced by their archrivals, Milan AC, the sports headlines had been calling her a 'Jezebel' and the 'American Delilah' who'd weakened their best player. Somehow the press had found out that she was three years older than Alessandro and that she'd been married once before. This seemed to infuriate the fans. Letters poured into the fan club, begging Alessandro to leave her.

Throughout all this, Alessandro remained aloof. He still took care of his weekly column in the Squadra di Torino newsletter and he ignored any reference to his private life. His coach had asked to meet Casey and they went to dinner with him and his wife.

Alessandro's coach, Francisco, was a charming man, and he and his wife put Casey at ease at once.

"We wanted to meet you," said Francisco. "You know, usually I never get involved with my players' private lives —"

"You *always* get involved," said Alessandro and Francisco's wife at the same time.

Alessandro rolled his eyes. "You wanted to meet Casey to see if she was really as awful as the press claimed."

"Well, I really wanted to make sure she wasn't going to pressure you into moving to America." Francisco patted Casey's hand. "But you tell me you have no intention of doing that and I believe you."

"You wouldn't believe some of the ruses the other clubs use to lure players away," said Francisco's wife, Julia. "I've heard stories of clubs promising Ferrari cars, luxurious apartments, all tax free…"

"And they hire actresses to seduce the players," said Francisco, waving his hands as Italians do when they get excited. "I wondered if you weren't an actress hired by some American club to seduce Alessandro."

It was lucky Casey had finished eating, or she might have choked. "I don't have anything to do with soccer clubs in America."

Alessandro grinned. "I know that and you know that, and now Francisco knows that. It's all right, Casey. We didn't believe you were an actress."

"Unlike someone else we know," said Julia, lifting her cappuccino and taking a sip.

"How is Gloria, anyway? She must be making a fortune with that calendar," said Francisco. "What a pity you didn't tell us the rights were for sale — the club could have used that fortune. We could have sold them along with the shirts, hats and banners."

"I didn't know they were for sale. I'd forgotten all about it actually," Alessandro snarled.

"Don't get huffy," said Julia, batting her eyelashes. "I bought one. Francisco is just jealous."

"It's hanging in our kitchen," wailed Francisco.

"It's amazing you even saw it. You *never* go into the kitchen," said Julia.

"Yes, well, the cook was making all these ooh and ahh sounds. I thought she'd just baked something wonderful. Imagine my surprise when I go in and see her gaping at the wall." Francisco gave a mock shudder. "Oh well, I suppose I'll get used to it. Besides, there are only twelve months in a year."

"It's not January yet. You'll have to bear with it for a few months longer." Julia finished her coffee and wiggled her finger at a waiter. "Another, please."

Francisco stared at her. "Another coffee? You'll be up all night."

Julia lowered her eyelashes and grinned at her husband. "All that talk about the calendar has made me want to stay up all night. Why don't you have an espresso?"

"See what you've done?" Francisco gave a theatrical shudder. "You've created a monster."

"On this high note, we'll take our leave," said Alessandro in a friendly tone. "I have to get some rest — there is another game in two days, in case you didn't remember."

"Oh, I remember." Francisco looked serious for the first time that night. "Alessandro, I don't have to tell you how important it is we win. My job, your job even, is hanging from a very thin thread."

"I know." Alessandro gave a rueful shrug. "But everything we've been saying to the press is true. The team is young and the players are still getting used to each other. We're making progress—every game is an improvement. The other teams took fewer risks than we did. We have a lot of potential that still has to be realized. The team knows it and I know it. Don't worry. We'll finish strong, you'll see."

"I just hope it won't be too late," said Francisco.

"*S'fortuna*," said Alessandro with a huge grin and an Italian shrug. "What goes down comes back up, and vice versa. Sometimes it's best to start with difficulties."

* * * *

Difficulties seemed to dog Casey all week. Her classes went from bad to worse as the students kept their calendars hanging on the easels and another rock sailed through her window in the middle of the night. This time she waited until morning and took it to the police herself, filing a report with Inspector Zucchini.

She went to the game with Jane Leeds, huddling in her jacket to hide from the crowd. Her knowledge of soccer was getting better. And although the game was so fast she sometimes didn't see what happened, she was starting to spot fouls and good plays. Alessandro was the pivot for the team. Casey understood why his fans loved to watch him play. Even if she wasn't an expert on soccer, she could still see quality shining from each move he made on the field. She felt ridiculously proud of him during the games. Only when she glanced at the hostile faces of his fans glaring at her, or heard the hoots and catcalls addressed to her, did her spirits plummet. What depressed her the most were the banners and signs telling her to go home — or worse.

She told herself it would get better — that the crowd would forget her and turn its attention to someone else — but, instead, they seemed to get more vehement.

The game was hard-fought, and as Alessandro had promised, the team did better. They were leading one goal to zero in the second half. The other team managed to tie, then Alessandro made a stupendous goal, putting the Squadra di Torino in the lead. They hung on to the last minute, and when the umpire blew his whistle, marking the end of the match, the stadium erupted in deafening cheers of delight.

Casey and Jane hugged each other, tears streaming down their faces. "Now they'll leave you alone," said Jane with conviction.

"I hope so." Casey wiped her eyes and waved to Alessandro jogging off the field. He waved back and blew her a kiss. At that instant, a cold silence descended on the crowd around them, and Casey, feeling the weight of hundreds of malevolent glares, got to her feet and hurried to the private exit where Tonio was waiting with the car. Jane came with her, shaking her head in exasperation.

"It's too bad people won't let you alone," she said when they were settled in the car.

"I saw the game. Alessandro played a super match," said Tonio, twisting around to look at them.

"Thank you, Tonio. Watch out!"

"Sorry!" Tonio swerved out of the way of an oncoming truck and waved his hand out of the window. "Idiot!" he cried.

"You were in the wrong lane," Casey pointed out.

"That's all right, he should watch where he's going."

"Right, since you're not," said Jane to Tonio. She grinned at Casey. "I'm so glad the team won. It's going to get better now, you'll see."

"At least Francisco won't be worried anymore."

"How was the dinner with them?" Jane asked. "I like Julia, don't you?"

"I thought she was really nice," said Casey.

"What are you doing tomorrow? Why don't we go shopping together? Mandy is in school all morning, I can pick you up, if you'd like." Jane loved to shop and she'd shown Casey some beautiful markets.

"Tomorrow my foster parents are coming to Torino."

"I'll go pick them up at the airport," said Tonio, speaking up. "Alessandro asked me if I would and I said it was no problem."

"Thank you," said Casey. "They'll be staying at the Palace Hotel. We're going to tour the city and Turin Hill, some parks, and we can also visit museums and monuments such as the Basilica di Superga where a mausoleum houses the remains of the kings of the House of Savoy." She let out her breath. "Does that sound all right?"

"You sound like a brochure." Jane giggled.

"I've been reading them all week, trying to think of ways to entertain them. I'm so nervous about them coming here." Casey wiped her palms on her knees. "I hope everything turns out okay."

"Will you take them to the National Automobile Museum?" Tonio asked.

"Of course," said Casey. "How could they come to Torino and not visit that? I'd also like to take them to Pralormo Park. I went there with Alessandro one day.

There are some great restaurants around there and we can spend the day in the countryside."

"I hope you're counting on me to drive you," said Tonio with mock sternness, "because you haven't asked me yet."

"I wasn't going to, you must be busy," Casey said. "But thank you for offering."

"No, no. I insist. What day shall we go to the country?"

Casey shrugged. "I was hoping Alessandro would be able to come with us. He's not playing until Saturday, so maybe Thursday would be a good idea."

"Ask him, but in any case, you can count on me."

"Thank you," said Casey. "I'm going to take them to some open-air markets, too."

"Well, there's the Bengasi at Piazza Bengasi, and also Madama Cristina in Corso Marconi," said Jane. "Those are the two I know best, but there are a few more around." Jane patted her arm. "Don't worry, Tonio and I will be on hand to help out. I know how much this means to you."

"And I know how lucky I am to have friends like you. Thank you," said Casey.

"I'm sure everything will be just perfect," said Jane with a reassuring smile. "And don't worry, they'll adore Alessandro."

Casey made a face. "That's what's really worrying me, isn't it? I've just been too chicken to admit it. I haven't seen them since I left for Italy, and they didn't want me to leave. Now here I am in Italy and I'm in love with another man. How will they take it?"

Jane looked sympathetic. "You're a grown woman now, don't let their feelings dictate your life." She blushed. "I hope I'm not overstepping…"

"No. You're right," said Casey. "You're perfectly right." She smiled at Jane. "But I really do want to keep them busy."

"Okay, Casey, here we are." Tonio stopped the car and let her out. "I'll see you tomorrow when I pick up your parents at the airport. Don't worry, Alessandro gave me the flight number and arrival times."

Casey shook his hand. "Are you going back to the stadium to get Alessandro?"

"Yes, after I drop off Jane." Tonio grinned. "I'm earning my keep tonight."

"Tell him I'll call him tomorrow, all right?" Casey said. She watched until his red tail lights disappeared around the corner then trudged up the stairs to her apartment. She should be thrilled to see Sam and Ellen. Instead, she was both happy and apprehensive.

* * * *

Alessandro was lost in thought. The Champions' League was about to start and he would be traveling more than ever. Casey would be left alone and he didn't like it. He wanted her to move in with him but she was being stubborn about it. She didn't want to talk about marriage, either, although that was all Alessandro ever thought about when he was with her.

He finished his massages then did some stretching exercises. The game had been tough and he was sore all over. When Tonio came, he was grateful to sink into the soft leather seat and relax.

After a few moments, he asked Tonio, "What is the matter with me? I have a thousand women ready to marry me in a second, if I wanted them, and the only one I want—Casey—won't even let me say the word 'marriage'!"

Tonio scratched his head. "I am not an expert on women," he said.

Alessandro sank deeper into the seat and sighed. "You're married and have three children."

"What does she say when you ask her?" Tonio asked.

Alessandro spread his hands. "She says it's too soon and that we hardly know each other." He made a face. What he couldn't admit, even to Tonio, was that just thinking about her caused his cock to stiffen to the point of being uncomfortable. He shifted a bit.

"A reasonable statement," said Tonio. "Give her more time. She'll come around. It took me a while to convince my wife to marry me. She thought I was too crazy to settle down. Look at me now…I'm as calm as a kitten."

"I'm also nervous about meeting her foster parents. They were her in-laws, too." Alessandro gave a little sigh of relief. That was better. Thinking about future in-laws helped unstiffen his cock.

"That is a strange situation…it would make me uneasy, too," Tonio agreed. "But I'm sure, with your charisma and bubbly personality, you'll charm them in an instant."

"Bubbly?" Alessandro asked and his eyebrows rose.

"I read that in a fan magazine," Tonio said.

"You'd better stop reading that junk," said Alessandro, grinning.

"What else can I read while I'm on the toilet?" Tonio laughed. "Here we are. I'll be here at six a.m. to take you to the airport, and no, I won't forget to pick up

Casey's parents at eight. You'll probably remind me a hundred times tomorrow morning anyway."

"Most likely." Alessandro yawned. "I wish Casey were here… That would make me feel better."

"See you tomorrow," said Tonio, waving as he pulled out of the garage.

Alessandro waved, then took his keys and opened the door leading to the elevator. He was tired. The practice had been grueling and he'd wrenched his knee a bit. He tested it gingerly as he walked. He had to take it easy for a few days, but tomorrow they'd be playing the Spanish team from Madrid and they needed the win. The Spanish team had been having a poor year and they were just as desperate. It was going to be a rough, tough game.

He poured himself a glass of Perrier, added a twist of lime and sat back in his deep leather couch. He flipped on the television and winced as Gloria's face appeared. She was doing an interview on Channel Five and she was—he leaned forward, the blood draining from his face—holding one of his calendars. That little pest. Now she was telling the viewers how she and Alessandro had been in love and how she'd bought the rights to the pictures because she wanted to be able to remember him 'for ever and ever.'

He turned the television off, exhaustion sweeping over him. Outside, the lights from the city sparkled and he gazed out of the window a moment. From his floor, he had a magnificent view over the gardens down to the river. Traffic was still heavy on the quay, even this time of night. Car lights lit up the river and there were one or two barges, their dark hulls moving slowly through the swirling water.

It was dark inside the apartment, but he didn't bother with the lights. Instead, he wondered what Casey was doing at this moment. Thinking about her made him hard, so he shifted to get into a more comfortable position. His cock thrust against the cotton of his pants and he reached down and stroked it absent-mindedly. His movements became more precise, as he pictured Casey in front of him, naked. In his imagination, she was stroking her own breasts, lifting them in her hands. He pictured her nipples hardening, turning darker, and with a soft groan, he unzipped his pants and grabbed his cock.

He put down his drink and lay back, his mind full of images of Casey. Now she was grinning at him, teasing, her tongue darting in and out of her mouth. Oh Lord. She turned around slowly and bent over, exposing her beautiful, full buttocks. No skinny twig, she — her curves were as luscious as a peach. He pumped up and down with his hand, his cock throbbing with lust.

He pictured Casey spreading her legs, teasing him as she bent over and spread her buttocks apart, exposing her luscious body to his view. He wished she was here with him, he wanted so badly to touch her, to rub his hand against her black, curly pubic hair, to stroke and lick her delicious pussy. He imagined her scent, her taste, the feel of her cunt pressed to his mouth. In his mind, he was plunging his tongue like a cock into her cunt, so deeply he could feel the entire slick passage as it clenched with her orgasm.

He pumped faster and harder. His caught his breath with a loud moan as he held his cock while his hot cum spurted over his hand.

Swallowing hard, he took a napkin and wiped himself off, all the while wishing it were Casey's lips and tongue doing the job. He squeezed his eyes closed. He had to stop thinking about that — he would only get hard again. Tomorrow would be difficult enough without him being exhausted.

Casey. He shook his head. She'd cast some sort of spell over him.

* * * *

Casey was a mass of nerves by the time she met her foster parents at the airport. She pasted a wide grin on her face, but her heart hammered.

Sam and Ellen saw her at once and waved, their faces wreathed in smiles. They covered her with hugs and kisses. "It's so good to see you! We missed you, darling!" they kept repeating.

In between welcoming them to Italy and telling them about her school, Casey helped get their luggage and introduced them to Tonio. He'd been standing to one side and had stepped in to take the luggage trolley from Casey. "This is Antonio. He'll be our driver while you're here."

"Hello, Antonio. Why, Casey, a chauffeur! We didn't realize you'd won the lottery!" Sam looked impressed. He was even more impressed when Tonio put the luggage in the back of the sleek car and helped them in.

Casey cleared her throat. Now that they were sitting in the car, perhaps it was the best time to tell them about Alessandro. "Sam, Ellen, there's something I want to tell you."

"Yes?" Ellen took her hand.

"I'm seeing someone here. I met him —"

"Oh, Casey!" Ellen didn't give her time to finish. "I'm so glad. Where did you meet him? Is he an art student like you?"

"No, he's a soccer player," said Casey.

Sam said, "An athlete. How nice. When do we get to meet him?" His voice was cool and Casey sensed his displeasure.

"Tomorrow — Thursday. We've planned a day in the countryside."

"We live in the country," Ellen said. "We were hoping to see the city."

"Oh, don't worry about that," said Casey. "I've got quite a tour planned. Here's a guidebook and a map of Torino — you can look at it and see what I've checked off. If you want to see anything else, just let me know."

Ellen smiled warmly. "That looks very interesting, thank you, dear. Why don't we go to the hotel and drop off our luggage? It's early, we can go have lunch somewhere nice and you can show us your apartment. We want to see how you're living. And, believe me, we're glad you've started dating again. You're too young to shut yourself in mourning for long. Two years is quite enough."

Casey relaxed. Ellen sounded sincere. She was also glad she'd resisted moving in with Alessandro. She could show them her apartment, then they could go have a walk along the river.

Ellen and Sam thought their hotel was perfect. After dropping off the luggage, Tonio took them all to a restaurant he knew near the Piazza Castello. Afterward, they visited the Palazzo Madama, in the center of the square, and Palazzo Reale and gardens, designed by architect André Le Notre. They finished the tour with a visit to the remains of the Roman

Augusta Taurinorum and the Museo di Antichità where they admired important Roman findings, including glasswork and silver from the Marengo Treasure.

"That was lovely," said Ellen. She leaned back in the car and sighed. "I'm exhausted. Why don't we go to your apartment, Casey, and have dinner there? We can send out for pizza or something, can't we?"

"Of course!" Tonio spoke up. "I'll even go fetch a pizza for you and deliver it."

* * * *

As Casey bit into her pizza, she sighed, "This is wonderful."

"I do love Italy," said Ellen. "And your apartment is very sweet. A bit small, but I suppose it's big enough for one." She paused. "I see you've hung up some of your paintings on the walls. Is that what you're doing in school?"

"Yes, we're working on landscapes. It's quite interesting."

"Did you do that one?" Ellen admired a watercolor Casey had done of the Po riverbank. "It's beautiful."

"Thank you," said Casey. She reached across the table and took another slice of pizza. "This is so good. I love the roasted peppers."

"Now, tell us more about your life here," said Ellen, dabbing at her mouth with a napkin. "You talked about your school and we met Antonio, your boyfriend's chauffeur. Do soccer players make enough money to pay for chauffeurs?"

"Actually, he makes quite a lot of money," said Casey.

"And we'll meet him tomorrow? I can't wait," said Sam. He finished eating and leaned back in his chair, putting his napkin on the table. "That was excellent. Thanks, honey, I had a great time today."

Casey was about to respond when, at that moment, her window exploded. She uttered a shrill scream, echoed by Ellen's cry and a shout from Sam. A rock landed on her floor.

"What happened?" Ellen cried, clutching at the edge of her chair.

"I don't know — a rock came through the window. Look, there's a paper on it." Sam went and picked it up. He tore the paper off the rock and read, "American whore, go back to your country. We don't want you here. Leave Alessandro alone." He frowned. "What does this mean?" He looked at Casey. "Is this Alessandro your boyfriend?"

"I'd better call the police," said Casey. She was shaking as she dialed the inspector's number.

"My poor darling!" cried Ellen. She hugged Casey and smoothed her hair back. "How awful. Why don't I clean up the mess?"

"I think we better leave it alone until the police come," said Sam.

"They'll be here any minute," Casey said. She was less scared than angry now. How *dare* that person throw a rock through her window while Sam and Ellen were here?

Fuming, she cleared off the table and put the rest of the pizza in her fridge. If she ever got her hands on whoever had done it…

She looked up as the doorbell rang.

"It's the police. I'll get it," said Casey to Sam and Ellen. She answered the door, peeking out before she opened it. It was Inspector Zucchini.

"Good evening, Miss Hatter," said the inspector as he entered. "I'm sorry this had to happen again."

"Inspector Zucchini, I'm so glad to see you." Casey shook his hand and showed him the rock. "It's the same as the other two."

"You mean this has happened before?" Sam said, outrage in his voice.

"Oh, Casey, this is not good," said Ellen, taking her arm. "You'd better come back to the hotel with us. We'll get you a room."

Casey was about to refuse — she was angry now, not the least bit frightened — but she stopped when she saw Ellen's expression. Her eyes were filled with worry for her. "I don't think — "

"You'll come with us. I don't want you here alone," Sam interjected.

"Really, darling, I'll feel better if you're not alone." Ellen clutched her arm tighter.

"Casey, I insist," said Sam.

The walls were closing in on her. She looked at the inspector, but he agreed with Sam.

"That might be a good idea," admitted the inspector. He glanced at the paper. "Same signature words as last time, same writing, too. I think we'll be able to find out who did this. I didn't call you before, but we found fingerprints on the last rock."

"Thank goodness."

"You changed your phone number, right?" the inspector asked.

"Yes."

"Why?" Sam asked.

"She was getting threatening phone calls," said the inspector. He shook his head. "I'm very sorry, Miss Hatter. I had hoped this animosity would have faded, but it seems to grow stronger. I saw the game the other night. The fans are quite hostile toward you." He looked at Sam and Ellen. "It's not every day the star player of the Squadra di Torino gets engaged to an American."

Casey sputtered. "We're not engaged!"

"Engaged?" Ellen appeared bewildered. "This is getting too much for me. My head is splitting," she added. "Can we get a cab to the hotel now? You're coming with us, Casey, and no arguing."

"All right." Casey felt a headache coming on, too. The day had been going so—now it was spoiled. She gave a resigned shrug. "Just let me pack my overnight bag. I'll call Alessandro tomorrow morning and have Tonio pick us up at the hotel."

"Maybe we shouldn't go with Alessandro," Ellen said. "I mean, you're obviously getting into a lot of trouble because of him."

Casey tried to be reassuring. "It will be fine." To the policeman, she said, "Don't worry, I'll lock up. Thank you for getting here so quickly."

"The police forensics department will try to get more fingerprints from this," he said. "We'll get in touch when we have something definite."

Casey and the Hatters rode to the hotel in an uneasy silence. There, Sam got her a room and paid for it over her objections. She was too tired to protest long and after hugging Sam and Ellen, she tottered into the room and sank into the bed. "Shower tomorrow," she muttered at the alarm clock.

It went off at seven and she got up and rubbed the sleep out of her eyes. Yawning, she ran a bath, putting some of the hotel's bubble bath into it. She sank into the fragrant, hot water with a sigh. After a while, her hands and feet started looking like prunes, so she got out, dried off and dressed. Last night she'd been too harried to bother choosing her outfit. She'd just grabbed the first thing she found in her closet. She'd wanted to look nice for her outing. Instead, she'd be wearing what looked like a school outfit—a short wool skirt in a Scottish plaid. She'd have to wear it with a red sweater and her white, short-sleeved blouse.

It made her look like a student, but so what? She stared at herself in the mirror and stuck out her tongue. Then she tilted her head. She looked like a schoolgirl, but a sexy one. The pleated skirt showed off her legs and when she whirled around fast, it flew up, showing her silk panties. She whirled again and bent over a bit so that her buttocks were exposed. She grinned and unbuttoned a few buttons on her blouse. Her lacy bra showed. Leaning over, she admired her cleavage. Her breasts were nice and round. She jumped and they bounced, almost coming out of her skimpy bra. She jumped harder and one did pop out, her pink nipple showing.

She unbuttoned her shirt more and pinched her nipple, feeling it harden. She rubbed it hard with her palm. Then she pulled down her bra and looked at both breasts. She ran her tongue over her lips. A pang of longing made her wish Alessandro were with her. He would reach up under her skirt, hook his fingers in her underwear and pull them off. Then he'd kneel at her feet and, grasping her buttocks, draw her to him. He'd press his mouth hard against her skin, his tongue probing for her clitoris, flicking it until she was so wet that her juices ran down her thigh.

Instead, she slid her own hand under her panties and touched her clit. In front of the mirror, she sat down and spread her legs wide. She tugged her underwear to one side, so she could see herself. As she watched, moisture started to glisten on the pink skin within her jet-black curls. She wandered her finger over her labia, the sensitive flesh changed color, blushing and swelling with desire.

"Alessandro," she whispered and she dipped her finger into her tight passage, slipping it in and out. "Oh, Alessandro." She groaned. She touched her clit, rubbing it until it stiffened. Her fingers grew wetter and she edged closer to the mirror, watching with feverish eyes. They were shiny with her juices and she put two fingers in, then three. Her cunt tightened and clenched. She gasped as it clenched again, harder, sending delicious shocks through her body. She leaned back on her elbow and bent her knees, spreading her legs wider.

In the mirror, she could see her fingers sunk into her cunt, her labia spread around them, her clit standing up stiffly, popping out from beneath its coral-colored hood. She'd never seen herself from this position before. It excited her even more. She wished Alessandro were there to see her so excited she was creaming. Her juices caused sucking sounds as she wriggled her fingers inside her throbbing passage. She thrummed her clit with her thumb, dipping in and out of her cunt, faster and faster as her breath came in sharp gasps.

The pulsation in her cunt intensified and her muscles tightened. She cried out as she came. Her breath coming in deep gulps, she stared at herself in the mirror, seeing her flesh contracting. She was drenched. Her labia were covered with creamy liquid and her hand was slick and wet. Her cunt pulsed in time to her heartbeat and she drew her fingers out and spread her juices all over her labia.

Shuddering with her release, her heart hammering, she stood and shakily rearranged her clothes. She splashed cold water on her face and brushed her hair. She leaned against the sink until she was calmed. Afterward, she sat on the bidet and washed herself.

There was still an ache deep within her, though — an ache only Alessandro could ease. She had fallen under his spell.

Chapter Eight

"I'm so pleased to meet you," said Alessandro with a broad smile. He waited a second then stepped back, a worried frown replacing the smile. The mirror reflected his pale face and the huge bandage that swathed his head made his grin look positively ghoulish.

He sat down on his bed and stared at his reflection. It was seven a.m. and Tonio would be by in half an hour to pick him up. Casey was counting on him. She hadn't said that in so many words, but he sensed her need. He wouldn't let her down. If only his head would stop hurting for a minute.

He closed his eyes. The game had been worse than he'd imagined it could be. A shudder ran through him as he pictured the stadium in Madrid. The crowd was immense—overwhelming. It screamed, and it was like a thousand jets taking off right beside him. It was a club championship, not a national championship, but it was important. In fact, it was the most prestigious championship in Europe — and fifteen countries fought like devils to win it.

Alessandro had gotten his first pass, and his first tackle slammed into his shins at the same instant. He knew then the game was going to be hard. Picking himself up, he'd called on all his wiles and skill to outplay the Spanish — until ten minutes before the end of the game. They'd scored and were leading one to nothing. Was that what had made him lose his concentration for a second? He never saw the player when he jumped, Alessandro's eyes on the ball, intent on heading it to his teammate Dario. His legs had been swiped out from under him and he'd fallen. Unable to catch himself, he'd twisted and had caught the opponent's cleated foot right in the temple.

After that, there had been a blur, when it seemed as if the whole world had tilted and plunged into a deep, dark hole. He'd awoken on a stretcher and promptly thrown up, which he hadn't done since he was a teenager and had gotten drunk one horrible night. An assistant coach took him to the nearest hospital. There, a doctor pronounced him fit to travel but said he had a mild concussion, which meant he had to stop playing for seven days. Seven days! The Squadra di Torino was scheduled on Saturday against Verona and he was supposed to play. It meant changing the whole damn tactic he and his teammates had elaborated.

He flopped backward on his bed and regretted it as his head felt as if a mule had kicked it. At least he wasn't stuck in Spain. For an hour, he'd thought they were going to make him stay in the hospital. But his X-rays had come back clean and he'd checked himself out in time to catch the last plane. He'd missed the one with his team, but he'd slept all the way home and Tonio had been at the airport to pick him up and commiserate with him about his head.

"Fifteen stitches!" Tonio whistled. "That must hurt."

"It does." Alessandro touched his sore temple. "Thanks for coming to pick me up. How did you know which plane I was on?"

"Francisco called me." Tonio grabbed Alessandro's luggage. "Come on, the car's parked out front."

"I owe you one." Alessandro sank into the seat with a sigh of relief.

Tonio laughed. "You owe me one hundred. Seriously—you look terrible. Are you sure you want to come to the country tomorrow?"

"Yes, I think Casey is counting on me. Pick me up at eight, before the others, all right?"

"Good night. Take care of yourself, Alex," said Tonio, his forehead wrinkled in a worried frown.

"I'll be fine tomorrow."

Famous last words. If anything, he felt worse. He prodded the bandage and winced. Painkillers—where was his medicine? There were the pills, stuffed in his pocket. And damn—was that the doorbell? It was. He groaned then tottered to the door. A day in the country could be a restful event. It might be just what he needed. Some fresh air and quiet.

"I'm coming, Tonio," he called. "Hold on." He opened the door and a cloud of perfume enveloped him, choking him.

"Hello, Tiger," purred a voice he never wanted to hear again. "I've come to make your boo-boo go away."

Alessandro put his hand on the door to steady himself. "If you really want to make me feel better, you'll get out of my sight before I count to three."

"Alex…it's me. Your Glorious Gloria." She stood in the doorway, her hands on her hips, her mouth turned downward in what she must have thought was a sexy pout.

"One."

"Don't be mean, honey," she whined.

"Two."

"You are going to regret this, believe me," she spat the words at him. Then, her baby-blue eyes narrowed to slits and she said, "I'll see you soon." She spun on her heels, her golden hair swinging out and brushing his face. The strong perfume made him gag.

With a sigh, Alessandro closed the door and sank to the floor. He reached into his pocket and fished out the bottle of painkillers. "A couple more of these might help," he muttered to himself, gulping them down. His head hurt so much he could hardly see straight.

When the doorbell rang a few minutes later, he felt a bit better, and by the time they arrived at the Palace Hotel, Alessandro had the impression he was wrapped in a thick layer of cotton wool. Tonio looked at him with a frown, but he shrugged and pointed him in the direction of the elevators.

"Sixth floor, rooms six-fifty-seven and six-fifty-eight," said Tonio. "Casey is here too. She called me this morning to say she'd spent the night."

"Thansh a lot," said Alessandro. He took the elevator to the sixth floor then stumbled as he got out. He straightened up and peered at the wall. *Why are the numbers so small? And why are they waving around like that? Is this the doorbell?* He blinked hard, trying to clear his vision, then pressed the buzzer.

Casey flung the door open. "Alessandro!" She stopped mid-stride and gasped. "What happened?"

"A kick," he replied. One-syllable words seemed to be all he could handle. Fine. He'd get by.

Casey peered at him. Her expression got more worried. "Maybe we shouldn't go out. Why don't you go back home and lie down? We can meet for dinner if you're feeling better."

Alessandro thought about that. He nodded, setting off another stabbing pain. "Okay," he said.

Just then the door next to them opened and a man and a woman stepped into the hallway. "It's after eight now," said the man. He caught sight of Casey and Alessandro. "We were just going downstairs to meet you." He hesitated. "Is this your soccer player?"

"So pleased to meet you," said the woman, shaking his hand.

Alessandro tried not to wince, but her words boomed in his head.

"What happened to you?" the woman asked.

"A kick," said Alessandro. He blinked. There were now two women and two men. Twins. He blinked again. There were twin Caseys, too.

"You poor thing. Soccer is a rough sport. I'm Ellen and this is Sam." The twins spoke at the same time.

"Hello," said Alessandro. He wasn't sure whom to look at. There were too many of them. He tried to smile but, for some reason, only half his mouth seemed to work. He shook his head, causing a stabbing pain, but the twins disappeared. That was better.

Sam wore an odd expression. So did Ellen. They were staring at him as if he'd just grown horns and a tail. "Um…you say you were kicked in the head?" Sam asked.

"Yes." The reply was short, but all he could manage. He swallowed again. His mouth was very dry and now he couldn't feel his feet. It was like floating.

"I think Alessandro will wait for us at his place," said Casey. "He's not feeling well. Why don't you go home with Tonio, we'll change our plans and go to the markets and the museums today. We can go to the country another day."

"Yes, that's a good idea," cried Ellen. She looked relieved.

Alessandro thought it was an excellent idea. He shook their hands, said "*Ciao*," and tried to walk back to the elevator. He'd taken two steps when the floor flew up and hit him in the nose. "No fair," he remembered saying, then he passed out.

* * * *

Casey tried to concentrate on entertaining Sam and Ellen, but she was mortified for Alessandro. He'd acted and sounded as if he'd been drunk, and although they'd found out he'd swallowed a few too many painkillers, it still didn't make him look any better.

When he'd passed out, they'd managed to get him onto Casey's bed and called the hotel doctor. The man was efficient and said that Alessandro was simply asleep and would be fine in a couple of hours. He suggested they leave him in the bed and Tonio had come to sit with him. Casey, Ellen and Sam had left to go shopping.

The morning had gone from bad to worse. Alessandro's calendar was in all the shop windows, advertised with lurid signs—most of them printed by Gloria so her photo was predominant, right next to Alessandro's. Then, when they stopped at a café, someone recognized Casey and there were angry hisses in her direction. Casey pretended not to notice, hoping that Ellen and Sam wouldn't hear — but they did. Sam got very upset and dragged his wife and Casey out of the café.

They went to a museum and there they managed to relax for a few hours. Casey was worried about Alessandro. Yet every time she mentioned him, Sam and Ellen begged her to change the subject.

"Darling, we really want you to be happy, but this is too much for us. We can't understand why you persist on seeing this person. He's a calendar pin-up!" Ellen patted her hand, a look of profound sadness on her face. "We care for you. You've been our daughter — our son's wife..." She sighed and shook her head. "I wish you'd come home with us, Casey. You're not happy here, I can see that."

"I am happy here, I have friends. You have to meet Jane, and..." Casey searched for something else to say, but she was too upset to think straight. "I am happy," she insisted, but even to herself, her words sounded flat.

Sam spoke up then. "You can't even go out in public. I saw that newspaper article this morning." His voice was shaking with fury. There had been a photo of the fans holding a banner saying, *Casey Go Home!* "You can't even go to your boyfriend's soccer games in peace. Your windows have been broken and you've changed your phone number. I insist you come home with us. Please. Your place is in Ohio, where you grew up and where people love you."

Casey stared bleakly out of the window of her taxi as it pulled out of the hotel's driveway. She had gone to get her clothes and to drop off Ellen and Sam before going to Alessandro's apartment, knowing he had returned home after waking. Sam's and Ellen's words had wounded her deeply, but the worst thing was – she *was* unhappy. She just hadn't been able to face it yet.

She'd smiled and hugged them before she left.

"We'll meet tomorrow at ten," said Ellen. "Come to the hotel and we'll make plans, all right?"

Casey nodded, her throat tight. That had always been Ellen's phrase, 'We'll make plans.' She loved to plan – whether it was for shopping or for reorganizing the closets. The phrase had become her signature. Now she was using it for Casey.

"Bye, Ellen. Bye, Sam, have a nice dinner. Do you remember the name of the restaurant?"

"Yes, of course. Good night, sweetheart." Sam waved, then the cab had driven her out of sight.

Casey gave Alessandro's address, then leaned back and tried to clear her mind. She couldn't leave Italy…it would be like running away again.

Outside the apartment, there was the usual crowd of fans and admirers. Some, she noticed, had bras in their hands and they were waving the flimsy scraps of lace around. Those were the worst – the bimbo fans – all they wanted was a chance to sleep with a star – they didn't even care who it was. Casey sighed. Usually they weren't out in such numbers. Tonight must be her lucky night. Too bad, she would have to go through the crowd.

She put on a scarf over her hair and a pair of dark glasses. That was no disguise. She was recognized right away and someone called out, "Casey, go home!" The cry became a chant and she was in tears when she got to the door. The doorman recognized her and buzzed her through. Behind her, there were jeers and boos, and some girls called out their opinions of her age, her weight and her chances of lasting one year with

Alessandro. "He'll dump you for another woman!" shouted one girl wearing a bodysuit cut so low it looked like her breasts would spill right out.

Fuming, Casey took the elevator then knocked at Alessandro's door.

Alessandro greeted her. His smile when he saw her erased all her doubts. She opened her arms and he came to her, laying his head on her shoulder. "I'm so sorry," he said.

"How are you feeling?" She drew back and looked at him. "You're still pale."

"I've been sleeping all day. What a mess." He grinned and shook his head, then winced. "I must have made a devastating impression on your in-laws."

Casey hugged him. "Don't worry about them. Did you eat dinner yet? Do you want me to order some pizza?"

"Tonio took care of all that. His wife went shopping for me. Why don't we just go sit down? I still feel dizzy."

Casey let him lead her to the couch and she sank into the soft leather and cuddled up next to him. "Do you want to watch television?"

"No, it hurts my eyes." He sighed. "I can't believe I have to wait a week before I can play again."

"You're nuts," said Casey. "Just relax. Why don't you go see your parents or something, now that you have the time?"

"Maybe I should." He shrugged. "I called my mother this afternoon, but she nearly deafened me with her cries when I told her I was injured. Never tell your mother you're hurt," he added. "She wanted to come right away to take care of me. I put her off, telling her I was fine, that it was only a scratch. But I feel much better now that you're here. I'll feel even better when we're naked in bed together."

"What did the doctor say?"

"About what?" he asked, with an innocent smile.

"Is it all right if you make love?" She watched him as she asked this. He blinked, but his smile widened and he shrugged.

"If I want to, I can," he said.

"Are you sure?" Casey asked, doubt creeping into her voice.

"The doctor made it very clear — I can't do it against my will or be forced in any way." He grinned, then closed his eyes and leaned back on the couch.

Casey studied him. His eyelids were lavender with fatigue and he had dark circles around them. It made him even sexier, along with the bruise on his cheekbone and the cut on his lip. His black, curly hair was nearly hidden by the bandage, but a few tendrils escaped, making his pallor stand out. His eyes fluttered open and he returned her gaze. An amber light smoldered in their depths.

He smiled. "Like what you see?"

"Hmm," she said, a teasing note in her voice. "I like. But I like it better when there are no clothes in the way."

He lifted his eyebrows. "No clothes? Just what are you looking at, young lady?"

"Your shoulders, of course," she said demurely. She batted her eyelashes. "Do you like my schoolgirl outfit?"

His eyebrows climbed even higher. "It is rather, um, cute."

She laughed and stood up, pirouetting so that her skirt flew up.

He blinked. "Don't move." He slid his hand under her skirt. "I hope you haven't been wearing this outfit all day," he said sternly.

Casey laughed and arched her back, bringing his hand in closer contact with her body. "I took off my underwear in the elevator," she whispered.

His eyes sparkled. "My very own naughty schoolgirl. Come here, so I can spank you." He pulled her over on his lap and lifted her skirt, baring her buttocks. His hand caressed her and came down in a teasing slap on her flesh. It tingled and Casey wriggled in mock hurt.

"Stop!" she cried.

"Is that a stop that means go, or is it a real stop?" he asked, holding her tight.

Her insides shivered. "It means stop and go," she admitted and she gave a little shriek as he spanked her again. This time it was more of a caress. His hand landed then slid down between her legs, parting them. With his other arm, he pinned her on his lap and his arousal pressed on her stomach. She writhed and his cock stiffened even more.

He chuckled and spanked her again, the sound like a clap. She struggled to get free, but it was a fake struggle. She loved feeling his hard cock beneath her and he was sliding his hand between her legs, fingers seeking her pussy. They found her, and, without preamble, one slid inside her. One hand held firmly between her legs so she couldn't slide backward, while the other came down with a light smack on her buttocks. She started to throb when his hand landed. The gentle sting drove her wild. She was getting wetter and wetter. His hand between her legs was now dipping in and out of her pussy, slipping and sliding with her juices. She moaned, aching for more of him inside her, then he spanked her some more, just enough to drive her to the brink of release. She shuddered against him, digging her fingers into his thigh. Her breath came in gasps. He shifted and withdrew his hand from within her. She moaned again. "More, please."

"Do you want something inside you?" he asked, pretending innocence.

She groaned. "You know I do."

"Do you trust me?"

"Yes," she said, wanting nothing more than to be filled.

"All right." With one hand, he parted her legs. Then something pushed into her. It was smooth and cool as it slid between her hot, swollen lips, and it surprised her.

"What is that?" she cried, craning her neck to look back. She saw her naked buttocks on his lap and his hand between her legs.

"A candle," he said. "Look." He withdrew it and she saw it was true. He held a white candle in his hand. "Smooth as silk." He kissed her.

She melted into his lips and as he kissed her, he slid the candle into her once more. He moved it back and forth, then up and down, tickling her from the inside. He used his other hand to undo her blouse and fumbled at her bra. His erection strained against her belly. He was as excited as she was. He grabbed her breast, massaging her nipples. The candle had warmed now and he plunged it in and out, faster and faster. The feeling was indescribable. She was burning with desire—the heat between her legs was building so fast it was like a brushfire. She opened her legs wider, rubbing herself against Alessandro's crotch, and he shuddered against her.

He tossed the candle away and dragged her up. He opened his pants and his cock sprang out, its tip nearly purple with need. She swung her legs to either side of his lap and impaled herself on him. When he sank into her, she started to splinter. Her body trembled as a mad shiver begin deep in her cunt. It grew — and she cried out as she came, contracting so hard her legs shook. Alessandro let out a hoarse cry, grasping her around the waist as he almost lifted her off the couch with the force of his orgasm. His hot seed shot into her so hard she felt it like a string of beads hitting her insides. She tipped her head back and let herself go — joining him in his release.

Afterward, they lay in a tangled heap until their breathing evened out and their hearts slowed down. Casey looked at the candle, lying on the floor. "What a great idea," she murmured, taking it in her hand. The wax warmed quickly to her body temperature. It was smooth and the base was suggestively shaped.

"It was a spur-of-the-moment discovery," said Alessandro. "I was dying to see something entering your gorgeous pussy...and this seemed perfect." He winked at her.

"I'll never be able to look at another candle without blushing," said Casey, a giggle escaping her. "I hope I don't get invited to a candlelit dinner anytime soon." The thought of the candle sent a pleasant tingle through her and she clenched her buttocks together.

"I want to be there to see your expression," said Alessandro in a teasing voice.

Casey sighed and snuggled into his arms. "How's your head?"

"It hurts," he said cheerfully. "But I feel better anyway. How about a shower, just the two of us?"

"That sounds like a plan," Casey said, then frowned. "What is it?"

"Nothing. I was just thinking of Ellen." She wrinkled her nose. She didn't know what to do to make her foster parents like Alessandro and it frustrated her. How could they start all over?

"She doesn't want to see me again, does she?" asked Alessandro.

"Don't look so sad. She'll come around and so will Sam. We'll have to think of a way that you can charm them. You're so adorable, they can't help but love you." Casey wished she felt as positive as she sounded. But she was sure that if they only got to know Alessandro, they would love him — or at least appreciate him. "They just have to get to know you as well as I do."

"Not quite as well as you do," he said with a definite leer.

"Ha! You have a one-track mind," she said, putting her hand over his penis. She loved the feel of it, hard or soft.

He sighed at her touch and snuggled closer to her. "I have an idea, why don't I invite them to a fancy restaurant. I know just the place. It's used to celebrities and it's terribly expensive, so there won't be any photographers or whatever springing out of the potted plants. What do you say?"

"Good idea." She stroked him, finding the satiny place she loved to touch just behind his scrotum. His cock twitched in her hand. She smiled at him. "You were saying?"

It seemed to take him a minute to gather his thoughts. "About what? Oh, dinner. How about tomorrow night? Saturday is the game and I have to be at the stadium all day. We're going to go over tactics with the team."

"And Sam and Ellen will be leaving Sunday. Well, tomorrow night it is." She put her head beneath his chin and rested her cheek against his chest. His heartbeat sounded slow and strong in her ear.

His arms tightened around her shoulders. "Tonio will pick you and your in-laws up at seven thirty. I know that Americans like to eat early. I'll take care of everything else."

She drew back and looked at him. "And you'll charm them effortlessly and they'll be so smitten they'll beg me to stay with you."

"That sounds nice," Alessandro said and his expression grew serious. "Casey...please, will you stay with me?" He got down on his knee and took her hand. "Move in here with me, Casey. Please?"

Casey was disarmed by his appearance. The bandage made him look fragile and his eyes were pleading. Her heart was hammering, and she started to tremble. "Can you ask me again after tomorrow night?" she said. "It means so much to me to have Sam and Ellen's blessing."

"Will you say yes even if they hate me?" he asked.

"I don't know!" She shook her head, her emotions churning.

"Don't you love me?" He took her hand. His eyes were filled with pain.

She pulled her hand away from him and backed away. Her heart was beating so hard it hurt her. She bent her head, tears starting to prick her eyes. "I feel caught in the middle," she whispered. "I want to make everyone happy and the result is no one is pleased and

I'm miserable." She looked him in the eyes. "*Yes,* I love you. Yes, I want to live with you. But I don't wish to hurt the people who took me in and cared for me. They gave me their love, they gave me their home, their hearts — and their son. How could I ever hurt them?"

"If you're happy, they can't be hurt," said Alessandro. He got to his feet and stood over her.

"You make it sound so simple." She sighed.

"It is simple." He leaned down and took hold of her shoulders.

"No, it's not!" she cried. "Look at what happens when I go to your games! When I'm on the street, I get insults and worse — someone pushed me into the road and it's a miracle I wasn't hurt. My window is smashed, the students in my art class hate me..." Her voice trailed off. "It's not your fault. I'm just feeling confused, that's all." She sat still for a moment, gathering her thoughts. "It's nothing to do with my feelings for you. I have to sort out my own life. Can you understand that?"

He gave her shoulders a gentle squeeze. "I remember what you told me when we met. You said you were feeling fragile. I understand. But all I want is to make you happy. I dream about waking up with you near me and hearing you running the water for your bath and humming as you look for something to wear. It would make me happy to trip over your shoes in my hallway and see your coffee cup sitting on the counter by the sink."

Casey took his hands in hers and drew him down on the couch next to her. She touched his face, tracing a line from his mouth to his throat, then she smiled and said, "I want to hear you laugh when you see something funny, and when you're sad, I want to comfort you. I want to walk with you in the sunshine, and when the moon rises above the mountains, I want to see its silvery light draw shadows on your face."

"We have things in common. You like gardens and golf, and so do I," said Alessandro.

"And we both hate shopping, we both want to live in the country someday and we both love to travel."

"So we agree with each other," Alessandro said, his voice gentle.

Casey's resistance weakened. How could she ever contemplate not loving Alessandro? "We agree," she said.

Alessandro nodded, but his face was very pale. "You frighten me, Casey."

She was startled. "Why?"

"Because of the power you have to hurt me. If you leave me, I don't know what I'll do." He spoke simply, but she heard the apprehension in his voice.

"Don't worry about that," she said, touched.

"I can't help it. I love you," he said, his eyes limpid.

Casey blushed. "I love you too," she said after a pause.

"You said you loved me. Did that hurt?" he asked, pretending to be a doctor and feeling for a pulse in her wrist.

She laughed and pushed his hand away. "No, it didn't." She kissed his nose. "I love you. *Ti amo*, Alessandro, *ti amo*." She said it in earnest, wanting him to believe her.

"Then never leave me," he said.

"It would take a very good reason for me to leave you," she said.

"Like?" he asked, lifting one eyebrow.

"Oh, infidelity. I don't think I could pardon that. I'm old-fashioned in some ways. And sloppy table manners," she added.

He grinned. "I will try to remember that."

Chapter Nine

Sam and Ellen were ready when she arrived at eight. They had their guidebook and their walking shoes. When they heard about Alessandro's invitation, they both agreed at once.

Ellen smiled at Casey. "Of course we'll give him a second chance. We thought about what we said and we're sorry. We're happy to go to dinner with him tonight." Her voice might have been a bit forced, but her smile was genuine.

"Well, now that that's settled, what amazing sights are you taking us to see today?" Sam asked, putting his arm over her shoulders.

They hiked all over Torino, managed to keep away from Alessandro's rabid fans and in the evening, Casey dropped them at the hotel.

Back at her place, she was glad to sink into a hot, fragrant bubble bath and rest a while. The phone rang just as she was dozing off.

"Hello? Miss Hatter? It's Inspector Zucchini. We have a result on the fingerprints and I wanted to talk to you about it."

"Oh! Hang on a second." Casey grabbed a towel, wrapped it around her soaking hair then shrugged into a bathrobe. "All right," she said, sitting at her table.

"We checked the fingerprints against the school records and found they belong to one of your classmates, a certain Angela Goty."

Casey frowned. "I know who she is. She's been nasty about the whole thing, but I never would have thought her capable of throwing a rock through my window. What should I do now?"

"Well" — the inspector paused and Casey heard a typewriter in the background and some voices yelling that there was an emergency on line one, — "you can press charges, of course. Or you can demand she pay for the damages, without formal charges. It depends on you."

"Do I need a lawyer if I want to demand payment? I've had some time to cool down since the other night and I don't want to press charges. It would just make more bad publicity. I think that if she realizes we know who did it, there won't be any more point of her throwing rocks. I'd like to give her a second chance, if you don't mind."

"That's probably the best idea." The inspector sounded relieved and harassed at the same time. There was more shouting in the background. "You don't need a lawyer. Just fill out a complaint and we'll do the rest."

"Thank you." Casey hung up, thoughtful. The girl was a pain, but she didn't think it was worth pressing charges about. But if she ever did it again...

* * * *

After drying her hair, Casey opened her closet and took out some dresses. Most were too plain for a fancy dinner, but she did have a dress that would be perfect. It was made of scarlet silk. The dress hugged her body, but the high neckline made it almost demure. It was sleeveless, but it had a long-sleeved chiffon vest that went over the whole dress, like a veil made of red smoke. The dress was knee length and she had a pair of gold high-heeled sandals to go with it.

She pinned her hair in a heavy knot at the back of her neck, with tendrils escaping and framing her face. She put on smoky-gray eyeshadow, with lots of mascara and red lipstick to match her dress. She had a gold clutch bag to complete the outfit.

Standing in front of the mirror, she tilted her head, admiring the effect. It wasn't vanity—she knew she looked good. She wasn't someone who would stand out in a crowd, but she had classic looks—good legs and high cheekbones, a long neck and a wide, generous mouth. She poked her tongue out at herself.

"Stop being so silly," she scolded her mirror twin. "You're just going out to dinner. It's not like he's formally asked you to marry him or anything. He just wants you to move in with him. You'll tell Sam and Ellen, they'll say how happy they are for you and we'll all drink some champagne and celebrate."

She caught a taxi and went to the hotel. Her budget was stretching to its limit. In the cab, she figured she had just enough left to buy tram tickets for the rest of the month and have enough left over for one package of noodles. She nibbled the inside of her lip. One thing was sure — if she did live with Alessandro, it would be easier on her budget.

How long would it last, though? He loved her and he'd mentioned marriage before, but she'd been so adamant in her refusal that he was backing off for now and hadn't brought it up in a while. Did he still want to marry her? What if she moved in and a month later they had a huge fight and he kicked her out? Where would she go then? What about the nubile women throwing themselves at him? She'd managed to keep her calm so far but Alessandro had so much sex appeal that most women would gladly… She shook her head. So far, he'd never given her the slightest cause for jealousy.

She wasn't a particularly jealous person, either, but then again, she'd had little experience in that department. David had been sweet. He'd been a serious, hard-working man who'd respected his parents and her. When he'd left on his innumerable business trips — sometimes for weeks on end — she'd never worried about him being unfaithful.

Would I have been jealous if I'd known he was seeing someone else? Casey sighed. She'd been happy working for the magazine, doing her illustrations, and hadn't really had the time to worry about David. Theirs, she realized with something like surprise, had been a sweet marriage, but one lacking in passion. Was passion so great, though? Was it enough to support a marriage? Years went by, bodies changed — would a marriage based on passion survive?

She knew she was just being picky. Her relationship with Alessandro was full of passion — but it wasn't built on that. She loved his sense of humor and his inherent kindness. She knew he'd had a difficult childhood, but he'd stayed close to his parents and growing up in poverty hadn't made him into a wild spender. His apartment was comfortable without being over the top. He only had one television, an economy car, and his wardrobe consisted mainly of chinos and Oxford shirts. He had ambitions of being a landscape artist and his bookshelves were filled with books on gardens and gardening. His favorite walks were through the famous gardens around Torino.

Casey shared his love of gardens and she even liked to golf, which was, he'd admitted, one of his favorite pastimes. So why was she so afraid of moving in with him?

She smoothed a tendril of hair back and straightened her shoulders. Alex loved her, despite the difference in age, nationality and status. He loved her. That was all that should count. A smile flitted across her mouth. She would stop worrying right now. They would have a perfect dinner, Alessandro would charm Sam and Ellen and everything would work out just fine.

* * * *

Ellen and Sam looked very chic. He had a dark gray suit, with a tie he'd bought at an Italian shop. Ellen had a simple cream-colored jacket with big gold buttons and an ocher skirt made of raw silk. Her gray hair was held back from her face with two tortoiseshell combs and she wore a silk scarf over her shoulders like a shawl. She'd traded her sensible walking shoes for a pair of elegant pumps.

"Don't you look lovely!" were Sam's first words to Casey.

"So do you two," said Casey.

"Where did you get that dress?" asked Ellen. "I haven't seen that one before."

"I bought it here. There are lots of second-hand shops in Italy — the prices are low and some of the clothes are amazing."

"It suits you," said Ellen. "David would have loved it."

Casey winced. "I'm sure." She wished that Ellen hadn't mentioned David's name. A pall fell on her good mood.

There was an awkward silence while they waited for Tonio. Casey was relieved when he came a few minutes early and as there was hardly any traffic, they arrived at exactly seven thirty.

The restaurant was classy — just one long room, with an amazing view of the city. Each table had a gorgeous bouquet of flowers, and silver candelabras held slender tapers.

Casey's face flamed at the sight of the candles and she was glad of the dim lighting. Ahead, the headwaiter was showing them their table. Alessandro hadn't arrived yet. But the waiter said, "Mr. Sottini called and said he'd be a few minutes late. He said to tell you that he had a last-minute conference. He'll be here in ten minutes."

"Thank you," said Casey.

"Would you like a cocktail or some wine?" the waiter asked.

"Some wine would be fine," said Sam, taking the menu. "Thank you." He looked around. "Very nice place. Your soccer star certainly has good taste." He scanned the wine list and gave a low whistle. "I don't dare order anything... The cheapest bottle starts at a hundred dollars! I don't know what we're doing here!"

Casey started to fidget. "Alessandro wants to treat you both to a nice dinner. Why don't you ignore the prices and choose something you like?"

Sam looked doubtful. "I'm not complaining, but I do like to feel comfortable."

"I wonder if we could have some mineral water," said Ellen, looking around. "I'm getting thirsty. Oh — is that Alessandro who's just come in?"

Casey swiveled around and gave a sigh of relief. "Yes." There was hardly anyone in the restaurant and he was able to get to the table without being stopped for an autograph or handshake.

"He still has a bandage on his head," said Ellen. "I do hope he's feeling better."

"He said he slept all day today," Casey replied.

"Except for this last-minute conference," joked Sam. He stood and shook Alessandro's hand. "How are you feeling?"

"Better, thank you. I hope you didn't mind waiting for me. My, um, coach called and I had some things to work out with him." He glanced at Casey, smiled rather tightly, she thought, and sat down in the chair opposite her.

Casey stared at him. His face was still pale and there was a new mark down the side of his face. That hadn't been there yesterday, she was sure. It looked like a nasty scratch.

"What's that?" she asked, pointing.

He touched his face and winced. "Oh, nothing. I must have cut myself shaving. Really, I apologize for being late."

"No problem." Sam motioned to the wine menu. "We were just looking at this. Would you be kind enough to choose for us? You know, we're typical

Americans... We know red wine and white wine, but that's about it."

"Which do you prefer?" Alessandro asked.

"Doesn't it depend on what you're eating?"

"Not anymore," said Alessandro. "The rule now is to drink what you like and the waiter will suggest wines to go with your dinner."

"Oh, well, maybe we should wait until we order," said Ellen, peering at her menu. "My heavens, there aren't any prices here."

Alessandro grinned. "The women never get the menus with the prices. It's a tradition. We're very big on tradition here." He waved his hand in a typical airy Italian gesture.

Casey hid her smile behind her menu. He was at his most charming, his smile wide, his voice warm — how could Sam and Ellen resist?

Playing the perfect host, Alessandro nodded toward Ellen's menu. "If you like fish, the St. Peter fish is very good. Otherwise, there is red snapper with sauerkraut, which is quite good, if you like that sort of thing."

"I prefer meat," said Sam, running his finger down the menu. "Ah, here we are. This looks good. Filet of beef with—" He was interrupted by a shrill laugh and all heads in the dining room turned as a blonde woman dressed in a sumptuous black dress wove in between the tables.

She was waving at their table, Casey saw. No, she was waving at Alessandro.

"There you are, darling," she cried, bending down and giving him a big kiss on the mouth. Her breasts brushed against his shoulder. She wiggled shamelessly, to better rub them against his jacket. "I was looking for you, you naughty boy. Luckily you told me you were eating here tonight."

"Gloria. What are you doing here?" Alessandro's voice was icy, but the woman didn't seem to notice.

Gloria? Casey thought she'd looked familiar. She glanced at Sam and Ellen. Their eyes were riveted on Gloria. Ellen seemed annoyed, but Sam's face was darkening. Casey swallowed. She knew that look. She thanked the heavens they didn't speak Italian.

Gloria let out another shrill laugh. "Well, I was worried. In my apartment this evening, you acted so...destroyed." She motioned her hands in the air dramatically. "Yes, darling, you were devastated. Our mutual friend Sonia...she spent the whole day with you, didn't she?" Gloria waited for him to say something.

Casey waited too. Who was Sonia? What had Gloria been doing at Alessandro's house? Why didn't he just tell her to go away?

Alessandro wouldn't look at her. Instead, he turned to Gloria and said tersely, "You know she did. And what of it?"

Gloria pouted. "You could have called me to comfort you. Instead, you only had a tiny little half an hour for me at the very end of the day." Now she turned and looked at Casey. In accented English she said, "I'm *so* pleased to meet you. Alessandro told me *so* much about you. Of course, he hasn't told you about *me*, has he?" She stuck out her hand and Casey was obliged to shake it, although she would have rather strangled the blonde woman.

"Of course he has," said Casey, in what she hoped was a cool voice. "He told me you bought the rights to his calendar. I hope the price wasn't too steep."

Gloria gave a dismissive wave. "What's a few million between lovers?" She smiled. "And he told you his rendezvous this evening was a last-minute conference with his coach." Gloria gave a little sigh.

"You weren't with your coach?" Casey asked Alessandro. It was as if someone had just punched her.

He looked like he was about to be ill. "No, sorry. I didn't think it would sound right if I'd—"

"If you'd told the truth. But the truth has to come out sooner or later," Gloria purred. "So sorry about that scratch. I didn't mean to hurt you. Gloria feels dreadful about that. I wanted to apologize."

"Why did you lie to me?" Casey asked, bewildered. "Don't you trust me?"

"He doesn't trust anybody," said Gloria, giving a shrug. "*S'fortuna.* That's the way he is."

"Don't say another word," snarled Alessandro, standing up. His face was deathly pale and he looked like he was about to faint. But he held on to the edge of the table and leaned toward Gloria. "Get. Out. Of. Here."

She fluttered her fingers. "She'll find out sooner or later. Bye-bye, lover boy."

Casey watched her leave, a sinking feeling in the pit of her stomach. "I wish you hadn't lied to me," she said quietly.

Alessandro nodded. "I'm sorry. I shouldn't have done that. It was…easier at the time." He motioned with his hands. "I would have told you, you know."

Casey licked her dry lips and darted a glance at Sam and Ellen. They hadn't moved, hadn't spoken, but Ellen looked nervous and was twisting her napkin in her lap. Sam was rubbing the back of his neck—never a good sign.

Alessandro sat down and looked at the centerpiece. He plucked a stray petal from the tablecloth. To Sam and Ellen, he said, "I'm sorry about that. Gloria was the one who bought the rights to my photos. You may have seen them," he added, his voice wry.

Ellen nodded and Sam cleared his throat. "Actually, we did see them," he said brusquely.

A red spot appeared on Alessandro's cheeks, but his mild expression didn't change. "It was a regrettable incident," he said. He shrugged and gave a faint smile to Casey.

Casey tried to return his smile but failed. "Who is Sonia? Why did she spend the day with you?"

"Sonia is Gloria's agent and lawyer. She brought over a ton of papers for me to sign. I refused. I wanted my own lawyer to check them out first. But she wouldn't leave until I did sign. I finally got my lawyer to come over at five p.m. He was furious, but then again, so was I."

"Oh." Casey didn't dare look at Sam and Ellen, who were sitting very still on the edges of their seats.

"Maybe we can order now," said Alessandro.

"You sound awful," said Casey, reaching for his hand.

"I'll be all right when I get all this straightened out."

"What exactly is the problem?" Sam asked, speaking up for the first time. He looked angry, Casey noted. But at who? Gloria? Alessandro? Or her, for getting them into this embarrassing situation? *Probably all the above,* she thought.

"I'm afraid it's complicated."

"Try me," Sam said, leaning back in his chair.

"It seems that... Oh no, now what?" Alessandro looked up again.

186

The headwaiter led a woman to their table and bowed. "Mr. Sottini, this woman has asked to see you." He stepped aside and an olive-skinned woman with glossy black hair sidled over. She wore a dress that looked like it was painted on her perfect body.

Alessandro stood, though it seemed to cost him an effort. "Sonia," he said.

"Yes." The woman was in her thirties. She had dark, slanted eyes, and her smile was blinding. She leaned over and gave Alessandro a huge kiss on the lips. "Thank you for this afternoon," she whispered into his ear, in English, loudly enough for everyone at the table to hear. "You were incredible. But, of course, you know that."

Alessandro turned red. "What are you saying?" he hissed.

"You forgot to sign this last paper," said Sonia. She shook her head. "Of course, you were in the shower and I had to leave. But when I got home, I saw you missed one. How lucky you told me where you were eating tonight!" She took a folded paper out of her small purse and smoothed it on the table. "Would you be so kind?"

Alessandro signed the paper and managed to turn his head when she kissed him — but she grabbed his chin and said, "Why act so coy? This afternoon, you were like a tiger." She waved and left.

The silence at the table could have been cut with a knife. Casey couldn't look at anyone. She twisted her napkin in her lap. That was a lawyer? Alessandro had spent the whole afternoon with her? He'd said he'd been sleeping!

Then she heard a soft curse from Alessandro. Startled, she looked up. A lovely red-haired woman was coming toward them. She was dressed in a peacock-blue miniskirt and had a bright yellow silk blouse. She was young, maybe nineteen or twenty, with the dewy freshness of youth. Her lips parted and she breathed, "Alex! I thought I saw you!"

"Who are you?" Alessandro asked. His face, Casey noted, was ashen and the scratch stood out vividly on his cheek.

"Alex, don't you remember?" She looked at Casey and pursed her lips. "Three weeks ago...at the soccer clinic."

Alessandro's eyebrows rose. "I assure you, I don't remember meeting you." He turned away and shrugged at Sam and Ellen. "I apologize, usually my fans aren't so forward." He spoke evenly, but his eyes flashed and he glared at the girl.

"Well, you might have forgotten. After all, it was dark." She giggled. "And I wasn't dressed like this. I wasn't dressed at all, actually..." She plunked herself on his knees and hugged him. "He's so shy," she said, ruffling his hair and smiling at Casey.

Her control slipped. She'd never made a scene in her entire life. She'd never screamed, had a tantrum or acted in any other way than as a lady—which is how Ellen had brought her up. She would not give in now. She heard rather than saw Sam push his chair back from the table.

"I think we should go," he said.

"Please, no." Alessandro pushed the girl off his lap and snarled, "Whoever you are, if you don't leave this instant, I will—"

The girl burst into tears. "That's what I get? You seduce me and then pretend you don't even know me?"

She sat on the floor, a picture of misery, tears pouring down her face. "You're a monster," she sobbed.

"But I never... We never..." Alessandro clutched at his head and groaned.

Casey was startled at how pale he looked and made to take his hand, but the girl was quicker. She stood up and threw herself in his arms again. "Oh, Alex! You're hurt! It's your head! It must be giving you amnesia!"

Casey could stand it no longer. Ellen and Sam were looking so horrified and she felt so awful. If she spent one more minute there, she would, in fact, make a scene. And she did not want to make any scenes. She wanted to keep her dignity.

She stood up and said, "Excuse me."

"Where are you going?" Alessandro said, trying to extricate himself from the young woman's arms.

"Home." Casey tried not to think about how devastated Alessandro looked, or how ill he seemed. She thought it would be better to leave and straighten everything out when she didn't feel like screaming or throwing something fragile across the room. As quickly as decorum allowed, she left the restaurant, Sam and Ellen at her heels. There was a taxi stand out in front and she got into the first one in line, tears blinding her.

Ellen hugged her. "Oh, honey, maybe it's not such a bad thing after all. I mean, you've only known him for a month and it's better to find out about these things early, instead of too late."

Casey stared at her, the blood draining from her face. "It's not what it seems, I assure you," she said.

Ellen wrung her hands together. "He's a star, Casey. It can never work. Believe me. We're just not from the same world. Please, honey, try to forget about him. I know you were in love, but it was just infatuation and that can't last. You should come home with us. You're so unhappy here. I haven't seen you so miserable since we lost David."

Casey couldn't speak. Tears filled her eyes, but she wiped them away with the napkin she still held clutched in her hand and she swallowed her hurt. "I love him. I can't leave. It's all a misunderstanding," she repeated stubbornly.

Sam shook his head. "You can't be serious? Alessandro has hundreds of beautiful women throwing themselves at him. How can you have been so naïve to think for a minute that he'd been faithful, or that he would resist? And even if he hasn't done anything—the day will come soon enough when he'll grow tired of you, Casey. You have to be realistic! He's a star and you're not even wanted here!" he said. "Back home people love you. We love you. We miss you. Please, Casey, come home. This is tearing you apart."

* * * *

Alessandro watched Casey walk out of the restaurant. Then he turned to the girl, now perched on his knees. His head was hurting so much it was an effort to see straight. All he wanted to do was rush out after Casey—but what could he say to her? He had to find out what had happened here and who was behind this fiasco.

"All right," he said, trying to keep his voice calm. "Who paid you?"

She looked hurt. "I don't know what you're talking about. Don't you remember me?"

"Your audience has left. Get off my lap this second," said Alessandro. He smiled. It was not a nice smile.

"I've never seen you before in my life and you know it. Now tell me, did Gloria pay you?"

The girl plopped down on the next chair. "Oh darn! I thought I'd get away with it. Of course it was Gloria. Who else could it be? She said she wanted to play a joke on you. She said you were stuck with a boring date and wanted to get rid of her." She pouted prettily. "I'm practicing to be an actress and Gloria said this would be a good test. So, did it work? Did I do a good job?"

"You did a great job of ruining my life, thank you very much," snarled Alessandro. He wanted to hit her. No, he wanted to hit Gloria. He'd never hit a woman in his life, but this might be a good place to start. He sighed and looked at his hands. He was not by nature a violent person and right now his head hurt too much to even think about sudden movement. Instead, he stood up and, leaving the girl at the table, walked to the bar. Slowly, because each step jarred his head. He asked for a glass of water to take a painkiller, then he called Tonio on his cell phone.

He felt numb and couldn't speak for a minute when Tonio answered. Finally, he managed to say, "Come pick me up." Then he shut off the phone.

The painkiller was strong and it made his hands stop shaking. When Tonio came, he felt a little better. "What a mess," he muttered as he got into the car.

"What happened?" Tonio asked.

Alessandro made a face. "Gloria was up to some tricks tonight. My guess is she's furious because I bought the rights to my pictures back—with a little help from Sonia, I might add."

"How's that?"

"Sonia was so involved in trying to get into my bed, she didn't notice when my lawyer changed a few clauses. She signed, I signed and I got my rights back. Gloria exploded when she found out—she came tearing back to my apartment and scratched my face in a rage. I got my rights back, but I have a feeling I just lost something more important."

"So why didn't you explain all this to Casey?"

Alessandro sighed. "I didn't get any time. Gloria sent Sonia and some stupid little starlet to the table to pretend I was cheating on Casey." He paused, trying to gather his thoughts. Pain was making his head spin and he felt nauseated again. The doctors had warned him about his concussion, told him he should spend at least three days in bed, without moving. But he'd ignored them, he'd made love to Casey despite doctors' orders and today's wrangling with Gloria and Sonia over his photo rights had wiped him out. "Mr. and Mrs. Hatter were there—looking at me like I was some sort of demon—and then she left. Oh, Tonio, I have to go see her."

Tonio looked at him and grimaced. "You look dreadful. What you have to do is get some rest and get better. You'll be able to set things right with Casey tomorrow."

"I won't. I'll be at the club at six in the morning and I'll be stuck there all night. At least until the end of the game and if we lose, I'll be stuck there even longer."

"Poor Alex. Listen, if you want, I'll go talk to her."

"No, you've done enough. I mean... Oh Lord, please make this headache go away."

"What time shall I pick you up tomorrow?"

"I can order a cab."

"Damn it, Alex! I work for you. Now, what time should I be at the apartment?"

Alessandro rubbed his head. "Five thirty. I'll be ready."

"That's better. Don't worry about Casey. She'll listen to you. Just give her a call and apologize. Women seem to like it when you apologize."

"I hope so, Tonio, I hope so." Then he was quiet as he looked out of the window. His stomach growled.

"Did you eat today?" Tonia asked, his voice worried.

Alessandro shrugged, then winced as even that slight movement sent stabbing pains through his head. "No. I didn't have time."

"And I suppose your refrigerator is empty and there is nothing to eat at the apartment?" Tonio shook his head. "That's not good, Alex. You need your strength."

"You're right. Stop at the Pescatorii." He wasn't very hungry, though. "Come have a bite with me?"

Tonio nodded. "All right. That's a good idea."

* * * *

Alessandro sat at his usual table, looking at his almost-empty plate. His appetite was slow coming back. He'd taken another painkiller and his headache had faded to a dull throbbing in his temples. He tried to dial Casey's number, but it rang and she didn't pick it up. "Damn," he swore, punching the number again and listening to the endless ringing.

"Don't worry," Tonio cried, patting his arm. "She'll come around. Let's see, I had antipasto for starters, then veal piccata, then cheese and salad. What shall we have for dessert?"

"Are you still hungry?"

"Aren't you?"

Alessandro shrugged. "I'm not sure. I think I've had one painkiller too many. I can't feel anything. I just want to go see Casey, but I don't know where she is."

"Try her parents' hotel," Tonio suggested.

"Of course!" Alessandro called the Palace Hotel and asked for Casey Hatter. The switchboard operator said there was no Casey Hatter at the hotel, so then Alessandro asked for Sam Hatter. The room phone rang and Sam's sleep-blurred voice came on the line. "Mr. Hatter?" Alessandro asked, clutching the phone to his ear. "Is Casey there?"

"Is this Alessandro?"

"Yes."

There was a heavy silence. Then Sam said, "No, she is not here. And even if she was, I would not let you speak to her. She's my daughter and you've hurt her very much. If she wants to talk to you, she'll call you. Until then, leave her alone." He hung up.

Alessandro stared at the phone. "No!" he said, his voice breaking. He looked at Tonio. "What am I going to do? I can't reach her on her phone and her father won't tell me where she is."

"Get some sleep," Tonio suggested. "You'll feel better tomorrow."

"*Alex!*"

He spun around, nearly losing his balance. A shrill voice cried, "What a coincidence! You just walked out on me at that last restaurant and here you are again!" It was the starlet with the red hair. What was her name, anyway? Alessandro frowned.

"What are you doing here? Why won't you leave me alone?"

"Don't you remember? Gloria paid me to go flirt with you and sit on your lap. Silly boy, you must have

194

had a big bump on the head!" She grinned and sat on his lap before he realized what she was up to. "She told me to follow you, so here I am again!"

A flashbulb went off and Alessandro swore.

"Well, I say, that's not very nice," said the girl as Alessandro stood and tipped her off his lap. She staggered and caught herself on the back of his chair. "Huh! Gloria didn't tell me you were such a bore!"

"She wouldn't, would she?" said Alessandro. "Come on, Tonio, we have to go. I have to get up early tomorrow."

"Spoilsport," cried the girl, pouting.

"*Ciao*," said Tonio, waving at her.

Alessandro thought he would be too upset to sleep, but the combination of painkillers and wine knocked him out as soon as his head touched the pillow. "Casey, come home," he whispered then fell asleep.

Chapter Ten

Casey woke up when the phone rang. She glared at her clock. It was five in the morning. Why had she woken up? Her message light was blinking on the telephone. A voice came on. Halfway asleep, she caught Alessandro's voice. "Casey, it's me. I've been trying to reach you all night." His voice was tinged with panic.

Casey groaned and grasped for the phone, but it was out of reach. There was a long pause. "Are you there?" Alessandro asked. "It's five in the morning. I have to tell you —" The message cut off. The tape must be full.

Sighing, she crawled out of bed. She rubbed her eyes then tried to push Play on the machine, but instead she hit Erase. Blinking, she tried to focus her eyes, but the ground tilted, dumping her back in her bed. "Too bad," she muttered, burying her head in her pillow. "He'll call back."

Her alarm rang at seven a.m. and woke her from a sound sleep. She got up and took a shower. She felt terrible. All she could think of was walking out on Alessandro and his stricken expression when she'd left. She'd left Sam and Ellen at the hotel, then she'd spent hours just walking through the city. She'd walked until she'd calmed down. Then she'd gone back to her apartment and found she'd forgotten to turn on the answering machine.

She'd switched it on before she had gone to bed, but when Alessandro had called so early, she'd been too groggy really to understand what he'd said. *Damn.* She and stared at the machine. "What good are you?" she asked it.

It was all a stupid misunderstanding. There had to be an explanation. A warning voice in her head whispered, *He lied to you. He said he was at a conference but he was with that Sonia woman.* She tried to still the voice. "He loves me," she said aloud. But why didn't he call? Why hadn't he come over?

Then she thought of the message she'd erased. He'd sounded terrible and said something about wanting to tell her something. He probably felt worse than she did. Well, she wouldn't let her pride get in the way. Hands shaking, she dialed his number and listened as his answering machine clicked on. She hung up before leaving a message. She didn't know what to say. Instead, she pulled on her jeans and a sweater and went to get her almond croissants.

The baker handed her the croissants and patted her hand. "We're so sorry about you and Alessandro," he said.

Casey sniffed and nodded, then jerked her head up. "Excuse me? How…how did you know?"

"We read it in the paper." He handed her the morning Torino news.

On the cover was a photo of Alessandro. On his lap was the same girl who'd accosted him at the restaurant. The one he'd claimed he'd never met. In this picture, he wasn't even in the restaurant where she'd seen her. No, they were in the Pescatorii, where Alessandro liked to hang out. The headline read, *Alessandro Dumps American, Finds True Love!*

Casey felt ill. Her teeth clenched so tightly her jaw ached. She handed the paper back without a word and went to her apartment. There was only one thing left to do. Pack.

When she could speak without her voice quavering, she called her concierge and made arrangements to return the keys. She hadn't given the three months' notice, so she wouldn't be getting her deposit back, but right now, she couldn't care less. She called her school next and canceled all her classes. Well, she wouldn't be seeing Miss Angela Goty anymore. She wondered if she still had to file a complaint, then shook her head. She was leaving.

She put her artwork in her portfolio, packed her clothes, and suddenly reality hit her with the force of a blow. She was going back. She'd never see Alessandro again. It was over. Oh God, it was over. She huddled for an hour on the floor and sobbed.

At ten, she dried her tears, called Ellen and told her she was leaving Italy. Ellen and Sam insisted she return with them, so by the time evening came, she was in a cab on her way to the airport. She felt as if the whole day had been a bad dream. Her emotions were so raw that everything hurt—her whole body ached. Whenever she thought of Alessandro, fresh tears filled her eyes. Ellen and Sam were so glad she was returning with them that she knew she ought to feel a tiny measure of comfort. But she was stunned. She sat between them, Ellen's arm wrapped around her shoulders. But her heart ached. She'd been so sure of Alessandro's love. How could she have been so naïve?

On the plane, she closed her eyes and tried to sleep, but Alessandro's face haunted her. Finally, she took one of Ellen's sleeping pills and sank into a dreamless slumber as she flew across the Atlantic.

* * * *

Casey pasted a bright smile on her face and strode into the kitchen. Ellen was making coffee and Sam was sitting in the chair by the window reading the paper. It was like stepping back in time. For a minute, she felt disoriented, as if someone had pushed a rewind button on her life.

"Good morning," she said.

"Sleep well?" Ellen asked, pouring steaming coffee into Sam's mug. "How about some eggs?"

"No thank you. Coffee will be fine." She had a sudden craving for almond croissants.

"What will you do today?" Sam asked, putting his paper on his knees and sipping his coffee.

"I'm going to go see Greta. She told me I'd always have a job with her. Then I'm going to the gym to see about taking classes. I want to get some exercise."

"Do you want to borrow my car?"

"No thanks, I'll take the bus." She drank her coffee then checked her watch. "I'd better hurry."

Ellen stopped her before she left the house. "You can stay with us as long as you like. This is your home, you know. We want you to stay here."

Casey hugged her. "I do know. Thank you."

"We hated it when you were so far away," Ellen admitted. "It made us think you didn't want to be part of our family anymore."

Casey shook her head. "I'll always be part of your family."

Before Ellen could say anything else, she dashed out of the door. She was glad to get away. The house held too many memories. They weren't unpleasant, but she was an adult now and she had to find her own place in the world. If only Ellen and Sam could understand that! The memories threatened to overwhelm her—sitting on the front porch swing watching the fireflies, David and her first kiss.

The scent of dry leaves assailed her when she stepped into the street. A cold wind slapped her cheeks. Soon the first snows would come and the ground would wear a glittering, white shroud. She looked back over her shoulder at the lovely colonial house on the corner. Why couldn't she feel at home there?

* * * *

Greta was as good as her word and Casey was soon working full-time at *Watch Out!*, illustrating articles and doing graphic art for the magazine and some of their clients. Her real love was still painting, but she had put all her art supplies away—she didn't have the heart or the time to paint anyway. Her days were busy and at night she went to the gym and worked out until she was ready to drop, anything to keep from thinking of Alessandro. Just saying his name hurt.

Ellen and Sam wouldn't hear of her looking for an apartment.

"Stay with us a little while longer, Casey," they begged. "We are so lonely without you and David."

Sometimes Casey wondered if it was emotional blackmail—Greta had been the one to put that idea in her head. But Ellen and Sam had raised her. She knew them better than that. They loved her and thought they were doing what was best.

* * * *

"How long, Casey?" Greta asked. She was typing up an article on drugs and her desk was littered with pamphlets.

Casey was standing near the window, looking at some slides. She paused. "How long what?"

"How long will you stay at Papa and Mama's house? You're a big girl now and you have to cut the apron strings sometime."

"Greta, that is none of your business." She looked at another slide. "This one is good. We can use this for the layout."

Greta sighed. "Stop with the pictures a minute. It is my business. You look so melancholy, it's bad for the magazine."

"I hate Christmastime."

"It's nearly Valentine's Day. Christmas holidays are over, sweetheart."

Casey gave a start. Four months? She'd been gone four months and Alessandro had never tried to get in touch with her. She shivered. The pain was still too sharp. "Valentine's Day?"

"Oh, by the way, I got a package for you." Greta pointed to a brown-paper-wrapped package on her desk. "It's from Italy," she said, pointing at the stamps.

Casey blinked. "When did that get here?"

"This morning. Why did you think I called you into my office?"

"To talk to me about drugs." Casey pointed to the article Greta was writing. "And to tell me how I should run my life."

"I never did that!" Greta said, pushing her chair back from the desk. "Well, what are you waiting for? Who's it from? Open it!"

"Greta! Do you think I'm going to open it in front of you? I'm surprised you didn't X-ray it to see what was inside."

"I would have if I'd had one."

Casey put the slides down and picked up the package. "It's from Ilario."

"Who?"

"An Italian journalist. I met him when I went to interview Alessandro." Casey paused, weighing the package with her hands.

"Well, don't just stand there. Open it!"

"It's a USB flash drive," she said.

Greta raised her eyebrows. "No letter?"

"No, nothing. Just the flash drive." Casey turned it over in her hands. "I wonder what's on it."

"Use the one on my computer."

"Right now?"

"Admit it, you're dying to see it," said Greta.

"Well, yes, I'm curious." Casey shook her head. Why would Ilario send this?

"It might be X-rated," Greta said hopefully. "Hurry up!"

Casey inserted the flash drive into the slot. "It's a video file," she said, frowning. She clicked on the file, then pushed the Play button and sat next to Greta.

The first image was of Ilario and his newscast partner, sitting in their usual seats at the stadium where they covered the matches. As the camera zoomed in on the two men, Ilario looked at it and began speaking.

"Stop!" cried Greta.

"What is it?"

"It's in Italian. Translate! That is an order!"

"All right." Casey rewound and started again, translating as Ilario spoke. "Tonight is the fourth match in the Champion's League. So far, the Squadra di Torino has lost two matches and won one. Here's our reporter on the field to interview Alessandro Sottini."

The picture switched to the field where the team was starting to warm up. Casey's heart lurched when she saw Alessandro. *He looks pale,* she thought. And there was still a scar on his temple. She checked the date showing on the screen. It was the tenth of November. One week after she'd left.

"Alessandro, this is the first time we've interviewed you since your injury. How are you feeling?"

Alessandro looked straight at the camera. "Casey, come home," he said.

"Hey, that was in English!" cried Greta. "Did you hear that?"

Casey was flabbergasted. "I heard."

The reporter looked taken aback. Casey translated again as he said, "Alessandro, can you tell us what your chances are against Liverpool tonight?"

Alessandro said, "Casey, come home."

Greta poked at Casey. "I don't believe it," she said.

Casey shook her head, her emotions churning. "Neither do I."

The reporter asked him a few other questions, but to each one, Alessandro simply replied, "Casey, come home."

Finally the scene switched back to Ilario and his colleague and they looked at each other. "What do you think about that, Ilario?"

"I don't know what to make of it," said Ilario, a frown on his face.

Casey and Greta stared at each other, but the video file wasn't finished. There was a break and the next scene was three days later. It was still the sports news, still Ilario reporting. He was at his desk now, reading from a prompter. In a deep voice, he said, "Ladies and gentlemen, welcome to *Channel Three Sports*. The big news today is the Squadra di Torino's win over Liverpool last Tuesday and tonight's win over Parme. Here to comment is Alessandro Sottini."

The camera panned left and Alessandro came into view. He looked at the camera and said, "Casey, come home."

Ilario coughed and said, "Alessandro, what do you think of the *squadra bianca's* new player from Argentina?"

"Casey, come home," said Alessandro.

"Do you think he helped the *squadra bianca* win against Parme?" Ilario asked, a frown on his face.

"Casey, come home," replied Alessandro.

Ilario made cutting motions at the camera and the scene changed.

Casey noted the date changed again. Ilario must have spliced together parts of different interviews. This time the camera was on the field again and from a distance showed a tired Alessandro limping off the pitch. In the background, the announcer was saying,

"Alessandro Sottini has just sustained an injury and has asked to be replaced. I hope it's not serious. Can we go ask him? Benito, are you nearby?"

A reporter stuck his mic into Alessandro's face. "This is Benito Flavi, live from the stadium here in Torino. Alessandro!" he shouted. "Is it your knee again? How do you feel?"

Alessandro paused and looked at the reporter. His face tightened. "Casey, come home," he said. Then he pushed his way past Benito and limped off toward the locker rooms.

Casey put her hand to her mouth. Seeing Alessandro again was overwhelming. Her heart was thumping so hard she could practically hear it.

The next tape showed Ilario interviewing Francisco, Alessandro's coach. "When will Alessandro be able to play again?" he asked.

"Not for another two weeks. The sprain was severe, but there was no permanent damage to his ligaments or tendons. His knee will be fine."

"What about the fact that he won't say anything but 'Casey, come home'? Do you have any comment to make about that?"

"I never get involved in the private lives of my players," said Francisco. "Alessandro's private life doesn't concern me unless it interferes with his playing. It never has, so I won't say anything except 'Casey, come home.'" He grinned, shook Ilario's hand and left the room.

Another scene. This time it was of the crowd. The Squadra di Torino was playing and the stadium was full. As the camera panned across the teeming assembly, banners were unfurled and the crowd started to scream. Only this time, the banners read

Casey Come Home! and the crowd yelled "Casey, Casey, Casey," as the players ran out to the field.

Casey put her hand to her face. It was wet with tears. She hadn't even realized she was crying until she'd tried to draw a breath and it had come out as a sob.

There was another interview. This time it was inside a stadium after another game. The date was February 10. The journalist snagged Alessandro as he tried to get by.

"Alessandro! You scored three goals for your team tonight—your first hat-trick in over five years. Congratulations! What do you have to say about that?"

"Casey, come home," said Alessandro, looking at the camera. Then he ducked and pushed past the journalist. The camera followed him as he walked down the hallway.

The tape ended there.

Casey sat stunned. Then she heard a sound next to her. Greta was crying into her tissue, her mascara running down her cheeks.

"You look awful," said Casey.

"So do you," said Greta. "Write to me, will you?"

Casey nodded. "I will." Her voice broke and she hugged Greta. "Thanks for everything."

"Go on, get out of here. And don't forget to invite me to the wedding."

* * * *

Casey packed, while Ellen and Sam tried to talk her out of going back.

"It's been four months—he never wrote, he never called, why go back now?"

Casey paused and looked at her foster parents. Their expressions were so forlorn she felt sorry for them, but her resolve didn't weaken. "You saw the video. I have to go. He needs me."

"So do we," said Ellen, wiping her eyes.

Casey hugged them both. "You'll always be my family and I'll always be your daughter. When I have children, you'll be their grandparents, so please, let's not fight now. I need you both, but I don't need to live with you. Can you understand that?"

Sam nodded. He blew his nose and said, "Well, I guess I'll drive you to the airport then."

"Thank you," said Casey.

"We'll come visit and you come back too — at least once a year," said Ellen, her voice cracking.

"Of course," said Casey. She put her suitcase in the trunk. "I'm doing the right thing. Trust me."

Chapter Eleven

The doorman tipped his hat when he saw her, and let her into the lobby. "Hello, Miss Hatter." His face was wreathed in a smile. "Mr. Sottini will be so glad to see you."

Casey's heart leaped. "Is he here?"

"No, he is at the game, Miss. The Squadra di Torino is playing tonight," he said. "Do you want me to leave your luggage in the storeroom? I'll be happy to keep it there while you go to the game."

Casey looked at her baggage and sighed. Then she said, "Is Jane Leeds here?"

He nodded and said, "Go on up, I'll call her and tell her you're on your way."

As soon as the elevator door opened, Jane shrieked and hugged Casey. "I couldn't believe it when the doorman called. I was just about to leave! How wonderful that you're back! Come on, let's go!" She took her arm to drag her out of the door.

"Wait!" Casey said, pointing to her luggage. "Jane, do I have time to take a shower? I just got off the plane and I feel so grubby."

"Hurry! I'll open your suitcase and choose an outfit for you. We're all so worried about Alessandro. He's been so upset. All he'll say is 'Casey, come home,' did you hear about that?"

"I did. Ilario Baldini played Cupid and sent me a tape on Valentine's Day."

"Go on! We'll have time to talk on the way to the game."

Casey nodded and dashed into the bathroom. She took a quick shower and the hot water drummed her awake. She'd been running on nerves for two days now and her head spun as if it were full of helium.

Her face was pale, but she had no time to do her makeup, so she dashed lipstick on her mouth and put on gray eyeshadow.

"You look stunning," said Jane. "What a body!"

"I've been working out." Casey laughed. She glanced at her reflection. She did look good. All those hours spent trying to forget Alessandro were reflected in her body. She turned and grinned at Jane. "What did you find for me to wear?"

"Jeans and a white sweater. You'll be in the team colors. Hurry now! Alessandro will be so happy to see you."

"I hope so," said Casey.

"I know so," said Jane.

* * * *

Jane drove fast, but not as fast as the Italians did. In the car, she told Casey how miserable Alessandro had been, and Casey related her four months spent working triple-time to try to forget her heartbreak.

"But I couldn't," she said. "Every time I closed my eyes, I saw his face. I wanted to call him a hundred times a day, but I never dared. And then the flash drive arrived."

"Ilario will have to be best man at the wedding." Jane laughed.

"I'll never be able to thank him enough. When I saw it, everything changed in my head. I finally saw myself for what I was — someone who'd never made a decision for herself. Everyone had always been responsible for me. But since I saw the video, I've changed. I feel so much more confident and I've become more assertive. Whether my decisions are right or wrong, at least I'm making them myself now."

Jane flashed her an approving look. "Well, believe me, this time you've made the right choice."

At the stadium, the guards waved them through and Jane parked in her reserved space. They took the elevator that led to the players' family section. Casey heard the crowd roar and knew the teams had arrived on the field.

"Here we are," said Jane, patting Casey's shoulder. "Come on. Everyone will be so glad to see you."

"My teeth are chattering," said Casey. It was true and her hands were like ice. She thought her heart was going to burst, it was beating so hard.

She stepped into the stands and heads swiveled to see who had arrived. One head, then a few, and a few more and a low whisper spread through the stadium. The sound grew and the wild cheering gradually hushed as it changed to a curious undertone.

The players sensed the change as well. They had been warming up, stretching, passing the ball back and forth and waiting for the referee to blow the whistle to start the game. Now they hesitated, slowed and looked at the crowd.

Jane pushed Casey toward the front of their section. "Go on!" she cried.

Casey walked down the aisle as if in a trance. At the gate, Francisco greeted her with a hug and led her into the players' section. She walked past their bench, unaware of anything except for a lone figure standing in the middle of the field.

Alessandro stood still. He was frozen, his face drained of color.

She blinked and tears coursed down her cheeks. She cleared her throat. "Alessandro," she whispered.

He started toward her. Walking at first, unsure, then breaking into a run. "Casey!" he shouted.

The crowd was preternaturally quiet. She could hear her own breathing as she walked toward him, her arms outstretched, tears glistening on her face. "I came back," she said as they met.

Alessandro swept her into his arms, lifting her off the ground and swinging her around. The crowd erupted then with deafening cheers and applause. The chant of "Casey! Casey!" was taken up by everyone.

She flung her arms around his neck. "Yes!" she cried.

"Yes what?" he asked, setting her down and taking her face in his hands.

"Yes to whatever you want."

"Are you back for good?"

"Yes."

"Do you love me?"

"Yes."

"Marry me."

"Yes."

He sighed and pressed his lips to hers. The crowd went mad, banners and white squadra flags waving. The other players gathered around, welcoming Casey home. Up in the crowd, some enterprising fan had crossed out the word *Come* and written *Casey IS home!* on his banner. Now, it flapped like a sail, held high by the applauding crowd.

"For our wedding, I want a candlelit ceremony," said Alessandro, whispering into her ear. Casey covered her burning cheeks with her hands and he threw his head back and laughed in delight.

"You are incorrigible," she said, kissing him again.

Then the whistle blew.

* * * *

After the game, Casey waited for Alessandro in his apartment. She unpacked her bags, hanging her clothes in his closet, where he'd told her—no, ordered her to put them. Her mouth curled into a smile as she ran a hot bath and sank into the water. *This feels good.* She was exhausted but she wouldn't sleep until Alessandro was lying by her side.

There was soft music playing and she'd lit the candles by his bed. All except one. The sheets were cool against her skin and she spread her hair on the pillow. She was naked, waiting for her lover to claim her. Her hands strayed beneath the sheet. Jane was right, her body did look fantastic. Her legs were trimmer and her breasts were even larger, thanks to push-ups. She tickled her nipples, pinching them gently, making them stand up. Then she dipped her hand between her legs, where thoughts of Alessandro were making her throb.

"What's this? A present for me...in my bed?" The teasing voice came from the doorway, then Alessandro stepped through.

Casey's breath caught in her throat. He was naked and his smooth muscles flowed like water as he strode to the bed and stretched out next to her. He grinned then fastened his sexy mouth on her nipples, moving from one to the other greedily. His tongue flicked them into hard points, while Casey ran her hands over his muscular back. He pressed his body close to hers and his erection slid up her thigh. She spread her legs, but he pulled back with a little groan. "It's been months. I think I'm about to explode."

Casey echoed his groan. "Me too," she whispered.

He cupped her mound, then, using his fingers, opened her. She was hot and slippery wet. She shivered at his touch and pressed closer. He chuckled, then his mouth replaced his hand and his tongue was stroking her from back to front, circling her clitoris and licking it.

She reached down and touched his head, digging her fingers into his silky hair. "Harder," she begged.

He glanced up at her, a mischievous grin on his face. "Do you like that?" he asked, his voice a purr.

"Can't you tell?" she whispered. Her body quivered at his touch.

Still looking at her, he pushed a finger into her cunt, dipping, curving, seeking her G-spot, his eyes fixed on hers. A rush of liquid warmth seemed to fill her as his finger slipped in and out of her tight passage. His eyes darkened. He lowered his mouth to her once more, flicking at her clitoris with his tongue. It throbbed, but an answering tingle reached her nipples.

She wasn't going to last. An incredible pressure was building in her body. It had been far too long and she cried out and thrust her hips up. His tongue flicked hard against her clit and his finger stroked deep inside her flooding cunt, rubbing back and forth. His mouth was still fastened to her, but his arm snaked out and took something from the bedside table, then she felt the cool smoothness of a candle sliding into her. It was too much. With a shriek, she let go, her orgasm shaking her from head to toe.

She clutched at Alessandro's hand, forcing the candle deeper inside her. Her head tilted back, she writhed against his hand, the candle's silken strokes penetrating her, his tongue still sweeping over her clit. The pulsing crested and was so intense she blacked out a second, her whole body convulsing with the force of her climax.

Afterward, she panted, trying to get her breath. But Alessandro hadn't finished yet. After kissing her pussy one last time, he knelt, then turned her over and drew her buttocks toward him. His hard cock nudged her pussy and she spread her legs to accommodate him. His breathing quickened as he thrust into her. She sensed him trying to hold back, but it had been too long. After a few slow thrusts, he quivered and drove into her urgently, clutching her, pulling her against him harder and harder, faster and faster. He arched into her, spurting, as he called her name in a hoarse voice.

His passion was contagious and Casey was cresting again. Her cunt pulsed along with him and she pressed her hand to her clitoris and stroked herself as her own orgasm took her.

They lay in a comfortable tangle, the moonlight shining in and outlining their bodies in silver.

"Give me five minutes," said Alessandro, sitting up and running his hand over her thigh, up her buttocks and onto her back. He stroked her, tickling her spine, dipping lightly into the cleft, following the narrow passage to her cunt again, where he teased the folds of her labia. "So sexy," he said and there was a catch in his voice. "I can't get enough of you. Wait five minutes and we'll do it again."

"Just five?" she asked, teasing.

"Or three," he said. He slid his fingers into her slick vagina. "Hot," he murmured. "Like hot silk."

Casey opened her legs, giving him access to her body. She was ready for him again. And he must have known it, for he uttered a soft groan. "Look what you do to me."

She looked over her shoulder. He was kneeling now and his cock was stiff, pointing at her. She grinned. "I think he likes me."

"Likes you?" He grabbed her buttocks and pulled her up to her knees. With one hand on her hip and the other on his cock, he pushed just the tip into her cunt. Sensitive from the last bout of lovemaking, she could feel the swollen head of his cock as it slipped into her tight passage, then he stopped. He moved it back and forth, leaving her body then entering it again with soft, sucking sounds. She was getting wetter. Her juices ran down her thighs. "More," she gasped, pushing against him. She wanted him buried within her, filling her completely.

"Oh no, this time it's going to last." He chuckled, leaning down to nip her shoulder. He slid his hand around front and sought her clit with his fingers.

"Touch yourself," he said. "Let me see you touch yourself."

She complied, thrumming her clit while he covered her hand with his. He grew harder as he pushed the tip of his cock into her swollen cunt. She savored each centimeter of his penetration. He slid in halfway, then, with a groan, he withdrew. Taking his time, he pressed in again, withdrawing just as his tip passed her tight opening.

She mewed with frustration and pushed backward, but he held her still, one hand clamped against hers and pressed to her cunt, the other reaching for her nipple. Her nipples were so hard they were almost painful. When he pinched them, rubbing his hand against them, she shuddered, her fingers digging into her cunt. He laughed and pulled her hand away. "Not yet," he said.

Casey's breath was coming in sharp gasps and his breathing was labored as well. She could tell he fought for control. After fondling her breasts, he put both hands on her buttocks. He held them wide open and inserted his cock into her cunt again, but just the tip. Leaving it there, he tickled one finger against her anus. "Do you like this?" he asked, pressing gently.

It was exquisite. Casey never realized she had such an erogenous zone. Just the light touch sent waves of pleasure rushing through her cunt. It clenched around his cock and he gave a soft laugh.

"I think you do," he teased.

"Please!" she sobbed, rocking backward against him. Being exposed like that, her cunt and her ass open to his touch and sight, was rousing her to new heights of awareness. She could sense every muscle of her body. His finger tickling her anus, the hard tip of his cock quivering just on the edge of her labia, were all magnified threefold. It was almost too much stimulation.

"I want to see your face," whispered Alessandro. He laid her down on the bed then, taking her shoulders, turned her over, brushing her hair off her cheeks with his hand. "*Ti amo, mia dolce,*" he said, his voice soft. His hands smoothed her hair then cupped her breasts. "*Bellissima.*" He swallowed, sweat shining on his neck and chest.

"*Ti amo,*" said Casey and was rewarded with a blinding smile. As he lowered his body to hers, she took his face in her hands. "I stopped the pill when I left."

He hesitated, the tip of his cock trembling on the very edge of her cunt. "Shall I use a rubber?" he asked. His voice was almost steady.

"No. I want your baby," she said and, with a soft cry, pulled him to her.

He gasped and sheathed his cock within her with one long, powerful thrust. He plunged into her again and again, lifting her off the bed with the force of his strokes. She cried out in sheer rapture, her body clutching at him of its own accord, feeling his cock jerking as he started to come, helpless to stop himself. He arched into her, driving into her sopping wet cunt, holding on to her as if he were drowning, crying out her name as he came. "Casey!" he shouted hoarsely. "Oh God, Casey." His body gave one last jolt and his arms trembled as he came.

Casey gave a singing cry. Her cunt was going to turn inside out with pulsing. Over and over, it clenched and throbbed. Her orgasm swept over her like a tidal wave. Afterward, her body shuddered against his. Alessandro clasped her in his arms. He held her until they'd both stopped shivering and their breathing had returned to normal.

The moon had started to set, but it left enough light to see Alessandro's face. She traced the edges of his mouth and jaw with her fingers. He stared at her, his heart in his eyes. A feeling of pure joy overtook her and Casey snuggled next to him.

"You have ruined me for anyone else," she told him, looking at his handsome face.

He smiled wanly, his amber eyes heavy-lidded with sleep. "It doesn't matter," he said, pulling her to him and kissing her. "Casey, you've come home."

Want to see more from this author? Here's a taster for you to enjoy!

A Polo Passion
Samantha Winston

Excerpt

Rennie went into the church to get out of the sun. Her face was burning. She'd gone to the supermarket to buy the weekly groceries for her mother and herself.

The church was blessedly cool. The darkness made it hard to see at first and her eyes took a few seconds to adjust. Then she slid into a seat near the statue of the Virgin Mary and put her groceries at her feet. She rested her hot forehead on her arms.

After a while Rennie felt better so she raised her head to look around. The church was old by Florida standards. It was made of wood and had wooden benches instead of the orange plastic chairs Rennie had seen in other places. The floor was wooden, too, and the church had escaped the worst of modern decoration. The statues were garishly painted, though. The Virgin Mary looked like she had on a bit too much makeup, and the baby Jesus, suspended dramatically above the nave, was bright pink from head to toe.

Rennie liked the statue of Saint Francis the best. At least she thought it was him. Her religious instruction, like the rest of her education, was sketchy. The statue showed a man holding an eagle, and Rennie vaguely remembered Saint Francis protecting the animals. The statue's face reminded her of her father's. He'd had a reddish beard and piercing green eyes, too. She noticed candles burning at the feet of all the statues and she went to have a look.

A card pinned to the wall read, *Big Candles 50 cents. Little candles 25 cents. Bless You and Have a Good Day.* It was a plain, white card. Nothing like her mother's new business cards. Her mother worked in a beauty salon in Palm Beach. Her business card, printed on shiny, pink cardboard, read, *Marilyn's Marvelous Manicures.*

"Rennie, your classes in that junior college are taking you nowhere. What are you learning there? I think you should enroll in beauty school," her mother had told her last week. "We could set up a business together. We could call it 'Marilyn and Renée's Beauty Shoppe'."

Rennie's real name was Renée, but no one called her that.

As she thought about the future, tears welled up in her eyes. She blinked once and they rolled down her cheeks. The bright Florida sun would bleach all her dreams right out of her. Her dreams of leaving the state, of going to a bigger university and getting a degree. Her dream of having a house with a real garden. And even the simplest dream of finding a job she'd like, not doing manicures with her mother or sticking curlers in some lady's blue hair. If only she had an idea of what to do with her life.

She looked up at the brightly painted statue and found her lips moving. "Help me, Saint Francis. Please. Help me get out of here. I don't want to be a beautician." The tears ran down her face faster and faster. "I don't want to be part of my mother's life forever." At these words, she felt cruel. That made her cry even harder.

Rennie stood stiffly, resolved to try to become a better person. She sniffed one last time and turned to the door. Her eyes were so blurred with tears she almost bumped into someone on the way out. Slowly, she started walking homeward.

"I will not daydream anymore," she told herself firmly. "I will work hard to earn more money. I will help my mother. I will think about beauty school."

She wiped her face. The heat of the sun dried her tears in seconds, leaving silvery, salty traces on her cheeks. She sighed and straightened her shoulders. "Only ten more blocks, just ten more blocks," she said.

* * * *

On his way to the tack shop, Juan saw a little wooden church standing by itself under two fig trees. His mother had been devout, he'd gone to Catholic school and his family went to church regularly. Although he hadn't gone to mass once since coming to Florida, he swerved his car into the parking lot and went into the church on a whim. After last night with the French brothers, Juan had realized how much he missed his mother and brother — he would light candles for them.

The darkness blinded him for a moment. Then he saw the girl. She was kneeling in front of a statue he recognized as Saint John from the eagle, and she was crying.

Her hair was the first thing he noticed about her — the color of sun-kissed apricots. It hung in a neat braid halfway down her slim back. She was dressed in cut-off denim shorts and a pale orange T-shirt that looked as if it had started out another color before being in a disastrous wash. Her feet were shod in plastic flip-flops, also orange, and faded.

When she turned around his breath caught in his throat. She looked like the Madonna his mother had hanging over her bed. The painting was old, Flemish, and the girl, by modern standards, was not beautiful. Her face was too round on the top and her chin too pointed. Her brow was high and pale. Her eyebrows were pale, too, like her hair, and her mouth was not the large, full mouth that was in fashion. It was small and folded like a flower. Like the Madonna in the painting, she had immense gray eyes as clear as rainwater. They were full of tears now, and red-rimmed, but her lashes were thick and dark. When she stood, he noticed she was tall and thin. Her arms were tan and pale freckles dotted her nose.

As if in a daze, she walked right past him out of the church and into the blinding sun. She smelled like fresh-cut grass and her hair caught the light when she walked outside and flashed red-gold. Then she was gone.

Juan sighed and walked to the statue of the Virgin. He lit two candles and said a prayer for his mother and brother. He tried to think of Rosa, too, but his thoughts kept straying to the slender redhead who'd been kneeling in the church. Why had she been kneeling in front of the statue of Saint John? He loved Saint John's the best of all the Gospels, but it was the most complex. He wondered at the significance the girl accorded to him.

Then his eyes were drawn to three large bags of groceries sitting under the bench. They were rather squashed, as if they'd been shoved there out of the way.

He thought they must be the girl's so he picked them up and went to his car. He would try to find her.

In the end, she was easy to find. Her hair shone like a beacon from way down the dusty road. She'd taken the second left-hand turn and was walking along the broken sidewalk with her shoes going clip-clap against her feet. She didn't walk so much as she floated. She stood straight, her thin shoulders pulled back by invisible wires, her head held high. She had long legs, tan and smooth.

He slowed his car down to match her pace and leaned out the window to call to her. "Miss! Miss!"

She glanced over to him but kept walking. He thought she looked nervous.

"Did you leave your shopping in the church?" he called.

At that, she stopped, a horrified expression on her face. She clapped a hand to her mouth. "Oh, no!" she wailed.

"Don't worry. I have them right here in the car."

She glanced to the left for traffic then dashed across the road. "Thank you so much!" she said warmly. "I really appreciate you coming after me. That's so nice."

She smiled and her teeth were white and even. Even her voice was delightful. Her hands were long and thin, like the rest of her. However, when she leaned up to the car window, he saw that her breasts were beautifully rounded, full and strained against the flimsy T-shirt. A wave of heat rushed through him. It was a strange feeling that encompassed her breasts, her scent and the color of her eyes.

"Do you live far? I'll give you a lift if you wish."

"Well…" She hesitated for a minute then smiled, getting into the car. "All right, it's not too far. Take the next road to your right, at the light. I live next to a chicken restaurant, you can't miss it." She giggled and the warm sound tickled his ears.

"My name's Juan," he said. "What's yours?"

"Renée."

"It's French," he said.

She looked surprised. "Yes, but everyone calls me Rennie. Actually, if you called me Renée I wouldn't realize you were talking to me. Only my father called me that."

Juan caught a trace of sadness in her voice as she said that, but didn't comment. Last night's conversation with the French players had reminded him just how painful the past could be, even when brought up with the friendliest intentions. "Is that the turn?" he asked, seeing a large sign with a red hen on it. The hen was dressed like a farmer holding a basket of eggs under her wing. The sign said *Den's Fryers*, and something about going Cuckoo. Juan thought he'd probably go loco if he had to look at that sign all day. He'd been brought up in a household where good taste was considered very important.

"Yes, thanks. Why don't you come in and have something cold to drink? It's awfully hot out," Rennie said as she gathered up her groceries. "I have iced tea in the fridge."

"Here, let me get those," said Juan, taking the bags from her.

Rennie looked surprised. "Thanks."

Juan followed Rennie up the steps on the outside of an old wooden house. It was built colonial style and had once been a large, single family home. Time had divided the house into flats and faded the paint and woodwork so that hardly a trace of the old mansion could be seen. All the doors were painted different colors now. Rennie's door was pink, he noticed. There was a pot of white geraniums near the door, with a bowl of cat food shoved behind it.

The apartment was cool—closed shutters kept the sun out. Potted plants abounded, some on the floor, some on tables, and the furniture was mostly wicker, with cushions in a light floral pattern. No paintings or posters hung on the walls, but there was a huge bookcase stuffed with books. Books overflowed onto the floor and were stacked neatly according to size. In a round bowl placed on a table, a goldfish swam in lazy circles.

Rennie put the groceries on the counter that separated the tiny kitchen from the living room and motioned Juan toward a chair.

"Have a seat," she said. "I'll just be a minute putting these away. What would you prefer, a soda or iced tea?"

"I'll have the tea," he answered. He sat in the chair next to the goldfish. The floor was bare, pine boards in the living room, linoleum in the kitchen. Everything was spotless. The apartment smelled nice, like flowers. There wasn't the smell of old tobacco. *No smokers here*, he decided.

He watched Rennie. Her movements were quick and decisive. Her hair was coming loose and tendrils hung around her face. Botticelli's Venus came to his mind—Rennie had the same grave look. She caught him staring at her and blushed.

"I look awful," she apologized. "It's this T-shirt, it's so old. I was just going shopping and, well...didn't think I'd be meeting anyone." She shrugged. "Here's your drink. Are you Cuban? I noticed your accent."

"No, I'm from Argentina."

"Wow! That's far away. Is it nice there?" she switched to Spanish and spoke with hardly an accent.

225

He grinned. "Where did you learn to speak Spanish?"

"In school, where else? Here in Florida we're mostly hearing two languages now. It's all over the radio and TV. I think it's great. I wish I could learn more languages. I'm taking French classes in college, but I'm not getting very far. Is Argentina nice? Are you here on vacation?" She settled on the sofa facing him, then she blushed. "Sorry, I talk too much."

"Argentina is wonderful."

Juan found himself telling her all about his life on the farm, and about his family. He spoke about his mother, about his father moving to England and leaving him and his two older brothers in Argentina. He talked about polo and the problems he was having with his boss.

Through it all Rennie listened with wide eyes. Clearly, she was fascinated.

Juan couldn't remember feeling so much at ease with a person, or being able to talk so freely about his family. Even with his fiancée, Rosa, there was that frown of censorship that marred her face when he mentioned his father. She thought he was a criminal to run away to England after his wife's death. Rosa only wanted to talk about marriage and children and how Juan would run the farm when they were married.

Rennie was especially interested in polo, and laughed when he came to the part about Andre's groom running away.

"He found someone right away, didn't he?" she asked.

"Nope, I saw him this morning riding his horses out on exercise and mucking out the stalls."

Rennie looked thoughtful. "I wish I could be a groom," she said. "I can ride and take care of a horse. Is the pay any good?"

When he told her, she gave a shriek. "Oh, please, please let me try! Introduce me to Andre, I'll work for half that, I'll learn quickly, you'll see, and work hard. Please, please? I promise I won't get pregnant and run away!"

"Are you serious?" he asked. His heart gave a strange flutter as he watched her face light up. Suddenly, the most important thing in the world seemed to be to make this serious, gray-eyed girl smile.

"Yes, a thousand times yes!" Rennie cried. "Just give me a chance. I know I can do it."

Juan nodded. "Okay, I'll let you try. You'll be on a trial basis for one week, and if all goes well, we'll hire you for the rest of the season until mid-April. But I don't decide. It's Andre's decision. All right?"

"Okay." She frowned. "What do I have to wear? Hardhat and breeches?"

"No, hardhats are only mandatory in England, although I think they're a good idea. Just any working clothes. You're going to get dirty. Can you come to the stables now?" he asked, checking his watch. "It's three-thirty, Andre should be there."

"Hold on a sec, I'll change."

She ran out of the room and he could hear her through the paper-thin walls digging around her closet for clothes. Soon she came back wearing jeans and a new T-shirt. Her hair was brushed and braided tightly and she wore low riding boots that looked old, in spite of the polish that made them shine.

She caught the direction of his glance and laughed self-consciously. "Aren't they sweet? They were my mother's when she was younger. Would you believe she used to be a terrific rider? You'd never guess now, seeing her, that she won a whole load of trophies. She had her own horse. Then she got married and had me. She gave me riding lessons for as long as she could afford it. I bet she's still better on a horse than me, even now. Here, look." She opened a drawer in the table underneath the goldfish and pulled out a photo album. She opened it and put it in Juan's lap.

In it, were snapshots of a woman dressed in impeccable riding togs and sitting astride a large gray hunter. They were jumping over a huge fence in one photo, and a couple of newspaper clippings, faded and well-worn, were taped to the opposite page. He turned the page and saw the same woman receiving prizes, or jumping fences, always with the same horse. He tried to see the resemblance to Rennie, but couldn't. The woman was a pale blonde with an austere expression on her angular face. She had wonderful style though, Juan could see that. She also looked familiar. He felt he should know her.

"Does she ride anymore?" he asked.

"No, not since I was born." Rennie sounded forlorn. "She had a problem when I was born, something to do with her back. She could never ride again." She stopped talking and looked away. Juan saw she was fighting tears, so he quickly changed the subject.

"Shall we go?" He wondered what Andre was going to say. He hoped he hadn't found anyone else. Suddenly, it seemed important to keep Rennie close to him. He wondered if he was developing a crush on her.

* * * *

Rennie was silent during the drive. Actually, she was petrified. She wondered what had prompted her to ask for the job. She'd never groomed before. She could ride, but she'd never taken care of more than one horse at a time. Juan had said she'd have six to care for.

Furthermore, how was she going to tell her mother, or on a more practical note, get to work? She'd have to take the bus, then walk through the club.

She was staggered by the size of it. They went through the front gate and Rennie goggled at all the mansions lined up along the drive. There were tennis courts and swimming pools everywhere. There were real gardens here, with rose bushes, hibiscus and tons of other flowering plants that Rennie couldn't put a name to. She'd seen mansions before, of course. Palm Beach had its Worth Avenue and the coast was one of the wealthiest in the world, but the polo club impressed Rennie. Everything impressed her. Arched bridges crossed the dark water of the canal. The landscaped gardens were beautifully groomed, as were the polo fields. There were huge expanses of perfectly mowed lawn with gleaming red sideboards running down their entire lengths. Rennie couldn't believe it.

Tucked into an endless orange grove, the barn was beautiful but unassuming. It was set amid four square paddocks and a tree-lined drive led to the parking lot in the back. Two other cars were parked there, as well as a pickup truck and a converted cattle trailer built to carry twelve horses to and from matches.

Two apartments tagged on either end of the stables, and the stables themselves consisted of a double line of stalls built along a corridor in the middle of the barn. Twelve ponies faced out toward the orange groves, and twelve faced the parking lot and driveway. Each stall had a fan in it, and automatic watering troughs.

Rennie found her throat was so dry she couldn't speak. She trailed after Juan as he went toward the east side of the barn and hollered for Andre.

A curly head of black hair appeared. *Is this Andre?* He had a friendly face under all those black curls, decided Rennie. His nose had obviously been broken before and had been set crookedly. He also had a wicked-looking scar that cut his bottom lip into two pieces.

"Andre, here's your new groom," announced Juan in Spanish as soon as he'd opened the door.

Andre looked surprised. "But I wanted a man this time, not a woman. Where did you find her?"

"On the side of the road," joked Juan. "Why don't you give her a try and if she doesn't work out, we'll look for someone else. The advantage is that she's American. No problems with green cards or work permits."

Andre shrugged. "Okay by me. What's your name?" he asked her.

"Rennie. Rennie Piccabéa. "

"Piccabéa, Piccabéa. The name sounds familiar," said Andre, wrinkling his forehead.

Juan thought so, too, and it suddenly dawned on him. "Your mother is Marilyn Piccabéa?" he asked, incredulous.

Rennie said, "Yes, she was. She is, I mean." She was surprised they'd recognized her mother's name. Nobody ever had before.

Juan nodded. "Of course. I didn't recognize her from those old photos. She was on the Olympic team. Those little trophies, they were silver medals. Her horse was the Sergeant, wasn't he?"

"Yes, that's right."

"You could've told me," he said crossly.

Rennie flushed. "Sorry, I'm not used to talking about it. We never do. Anyway, it was a long time ago."

"How old are you?" Juan asked.

"Twenty-one."

Juan tapped his chin pensively. "I don't remember her, but my father was on the English jumping team and he used to talk about your mother when he spoke about the Olympics. He never knew why she stopped..."

Rennie tightened her lips. "It was because of me," she reminded him. "I was a breech birth and it hurt my mother's back."

Juan noticed the set of her mouth. "Sorry."

Rennie sighed. "It's okay. She married her trainer right after the Olympics. Then she had me."

"Your father was her trainer?" asked Andre. He sounded amused.

"For a while. Then he had an accident and died. My mother says we're cursed," she added, looking suddenly worried.

"Poor kid!" said Andre. "Well, I don't believe in curses. You can start tomorrow at five a.m. I'll show you around now and tell you what's to be done. The horses are all pretty good, except Pinto, the paint pony. He's green." He turned and pointed to a truck. "That's the grooms' pickup, you can use that. You have a driver's license, don't you?"

Sign up for our newsletter and find out about all our romance book releases, eBook sales and promotions, sneak peeks and FREE romance books!

About the Author

Samantha Winston is the pen name for sci-fi writer Jennifer Macaire. She lives in France with her husband, children, and two dogs. She grew up in upstate New York, Samoa, and the Virgin Islands. She graduated and moved to NYC where she modelled for five years for Elite. She went to France and met her husband at the polo club. All that is true. But she mostly likes to make up stories.

Samantha loves to hear from readers. You can find her contact information, website details and author profile page at http://www.totallybound.com